THE MISTAKE

THE MISTAKE

Marilyn DeMars

iUniverse, Inc.
New York Lincoln Shanghai

The Mistake

Copyright © 2006 by Marilyn M. DeMars

All rights reserved. No part of this book may be used or reproduced by any means, graphic, electronic, or mechanical, including photocopying, recording, taping or by any information storage retrieval system without the written permission of the publisher except in the case of brief quotations embodied in critical articles and reviews.

iUniverse books may be ordered through booksellers or by contacting:

iUniverse
2021 Pine Lake Road, Suite 100
Lincoln, NE 68512
www.iuniverse.com
1-800-Authors (1-800-288-4677)

This is a work of fiction. All of the characters, names, incidents, organizations and dialogue in this novel are either the products of the author's imagination or are used fictitiously.

ISBN-13: 978-0-595-40665-4 (pbk)
ISBN-13: 978-0-595-85031-0 (ebk)
ISBN-10: 0-595-40665-3 (pbk)
ISBN-10: 0-595-85031-6 (ebk)

Printed in the United States of America

CHAPTER 1

It was mandatory. All fifteen employees of Milo Printing had been required to stay for the Friday night after-hours party in the lunchroom. In addition to it being the company's ten-year anniversary the owner, John Milo, said he was going to make a special announcement that would affect everyone.

A tasty chicken dinner had been catered, a self-serve bar was set up in the corner, and music played from a stereo. Though Carla Wade was not a drinker, she found herself indulging tonight in a special concoction that Marty Wilson, Milo's accountant, kept mixing up for her. Unknown as the contents were to her, the taste was amazingly good and helped ease the resentment she had toward having to be there when there was someplace else she'd rather be.

She and Darcy Lucas stood chatting and sipping their third drinks since dinner. The two women were best friends as well as coworkers and together had run the service counter at Milo Printing from the very start of the company. The years had been good to them, both in their work and in their relationship.

While Carla was a honey-blonde with blue eyes and a serene nature, Darcy, in contrast, was dark-haired, dark-eyed and brazen. Being the only women employees at the small printing company, the two of them were credited by the men for lending an interesting balance to the place.

"Wonder what the big announcement is going to be," Darcy said, speaking Carla's exact thought.

"Guess we'll soon find out." Carla glanced at the wall clock. It was eight ten. Surely John Milo wouldn't keep his employees in suspense much longer.

"Yeah," Darcy laughed, "now that he's got us all stuffed, sloshed and ready for the kill."

"It could be *good* news," Carla said.

"I suppose it *could* be," Darcy scoffed, "but behind the niceties it sure feels to me more like we're being set up for a raw deal."

Carla frowned. "Raw deal?"

"We're a small company in a big world. Wouldn't surprise me if Milo's decided to hang it up against his competition."

Change didn't come easily for Carla. She loved the simple, predictable life she led in the small town of Tag Lake, Minnesota. Sameness was her comfort zone. The thought of what could possibly be happening to Milo Printing had her feeling apprehensive.

Ready for another drink, she gave her empty glass to Marty and he gallantly mixed her a refill. He seemed good at bartending. Though he was also making drinks for some of the others at the party, he claimed his specialty was only for her and her alone.

"One of a kind," he told Carla, "just like you."

His line was lame, but she was hooked on his drinks.

"Hey, you two." Alonzo Quinn, from the print shop, joined the women.

He was somewhere in his late thirties, as were Carla and Darcy. A good-looking guy, with smoldering Latin eyes and a beguiling voice that said much in few words. Carla'd never gotten to know him very well in the six months he'd worked at Milo. Actually, she'd somehow always felt a little unsettled in his presence.

Darcy, on the other hand, always bubbled at his appearance. "Hey, yourself," she said, clinking her glass to his.

"What are you girls drinking?" Alonzo asked.

Carla gave a demure shrug. "I don't know what's in mine, only that it's called a Marty's special."

"Ahh…" Alonzo warned, "sounds like something you may hate him for in the morning."

"She will," Darcy said. "Carla normally doesn't drink at all."

Alonzo smiled. "Ahh…then she may likely hate the whole world tomorrow."

Carla caught herself looking way too deeply into those alluring eyes of his and immediately lowered her gaze. He had this disarming effect on her, which she imagined he had on all women. Except probably for Darcy, who outwardly preferred being the disarmer rather than the disarmed.

Darcy slipped her arm around Alonzo's waist. "Why don't we have Marty mix you up something better than just that beer you're drinking. Like one of my vodka sours for instance."

Alonzo smiled graciously and took a step back from her, saying, "No thanks, beer's working just fine for me."

"Working?" Carla questioned.

Darcy beat him to an explanation. "He's getting just as intoxicated on beer as he would on the hard stuff."

"No, no," Alonzo said defensively, "I never get drunk, just relaxed."

Darcy raised her eyebrows and laughed. "You're one hell of a perfect guy, you know that? A man who drinks like a gentleman…my, my, aren't you the rare one." She had a knack for pushing compliments into annoyance, and Alonzo was definitely looking pushed.

"Oh, I *love* this song," Carla purposely changed the subject for his benefit.

Alonzo took special notice of Neil Diamond's *Play Me*. It was a soft deviation from the consecutive rock numbers that had been playing. Looking as if he loved it as well, he asked her, "Care to dance?"

Carla didn't believe her ears. *Did he just ask me to dance?* She looked at Darcy, who stood there in her own disbelief, then back at this guy from the print shop.

Without waiting for Carla's answer, Alonzo took her drink away from her, set it on a table, and escorted her to the center of the lunchroom.

Carla couldn't remember the last time she'd danced. Like forever. But Alonzo's adept lead made it seem as if they'd danced together a hundred times. His hand on her back felt warm and confident, and her hand on his shoulder felt natural. Their close bodies moved in time to Diamond's sweet song.

It became easier for Carla to hold eye contact with Alonzo. She no longer looked away the moment he smiled at her. She smiled right back at him. And when he lowered his gaze in observance of more than just her face, she felt shamelessly sexy in her beige knit dress. Besides the great color, the bodice was scoop-necked and smoothly fitted, and the skirt transcended to a soft, knee-length flare. Though she'd always felt good in this dress, she'd never felt as sensual.

Carla's hand left Alonzo's shoulder and slid to his neck where her fingers couldn't wait to play with the ends of his longish hair. Soon becoming consciously aware of being watched by others in the room, she realized how much she'd stepped out of her usual self. She'd become infatuated by the magical combination of music, drinks, and dance. And too infatuated to really care how it looked. She was totally lost in the moment. And in Alonzo, who was so much more than she'd ever imagined him to be.

Suddenly the music stopped and the lunchroom turned silent. John Milo was ready to make his announcement.

"Great party, don't you think?" the handsome fifty-year old began. He waited while everyone clapped in agreement, then he proceeded. "Thanks to all of you for being here. Thanks to all of you for being such good employees. Some of you have been here since the beginning, some of you not so long. But we're a good team, all of us together. I wanted everyone to be here tonight as part of this ten-year celebration. You're my second family, really."

Coming to stand beside Carla, Darcy whispered, "Here comes the guilt trip, and I suppose he—"

Carla put a finger to her lips to shush her.

"As all of you know," Milo continued, "change comes often in today's world. Good ones and bad ones. Our company is about to make a good one."

Carla glanced at Alonzo, standing at her other side, finding him also looking back at her rather than at John Milo. They shared a smile that dreamily made it seem as if they were still dancing. But they weren't. They were only trying to listen to a speech from their boss while being helplessly distracted by each other like a couple of self-absorbed teenagers.

Carla stepped away from the group in search of her drink. She found it, took it, and drank what was left of it. Standing apart from the others, she tried to concentrate on the actual purpose of the party. The purpose…the purpose…

John Milo spoke with enthusiastic vigor. "We just locked up a huge contract from Tomlins, over in Redwood Falls. I mean, *huge*! Which urged me to realize that Milo Printing needs to grow with the times. First of all we need more space. So I bought that vacant Gantly building on the corner of Logan and Main. It's bigger and better than this place and will accommodate the new equipment I intend to buy. This upgrading will begin as soon as the first of next month. As a part of that, you're all getting raises and there'll be some additional people hired. So that's it, gang! Something I thought we should all celebrate together. What'dya say?"

Milo's staff clapped and cheered. The news set well. Milo Printing wasn't going under, it was only going a few blocks down the street to provide for its success.

There was a question and answer session, then some additional partying, and eventually employees one by one began leaving. Nice music was still playing.

"Another dance?" Alonzo asked Carla.

"I, uh…I…" she stuttered awkwardly.

Darcy's voice was steadier, "I should take you home, Carla. You're looking mighty strange."

"I…it's just that…" Carla laughed at herself, "I'm surprised at Milo's news. I mean, after having imagined the worse."

"At least we've got our jobs," Darcy scowled. "Even though we had to give up a perfectly good Friday night just to hear it. Oh well, come on, Carla, let's get you home."

"Maybe somebody should drive *you* home," Alonzo suggested to Darcy.

She smiled mischievously at him. "You offering?"

"Oh for heaven's sake, Darcy!" Carla said in an outburst that shocked herself even more than Darcy and Alonzo. Then more subdued, she added, "I'm fine, Alonzo's fine, you're fine, everyone's fine, so just take care of yourself and go, okay?"

Darcy seemed a little beside herself for a moment. But then she gave Carla a hug, said good night to Alonzo, and left.

As Carla and Alonzo stood side by side, exchanging parting words with the last of those leaving, it was almost as if they'd been the evening's host and hostess.

On John Milo's way out he turned off the stereo and told them, "Come on, you two, call it a day like the rest of us. Go home, have a good weekend, see ya Monday."

"There's still some food and stuff to put away," Alonzo noted. "Carla and I…we can clean up a bit before leaving."

Milo looked at Carla. When she nodded, he laughed and said, "Well, okay, if you guys want to, thanks. Good night."

The door leading to the back parking lot closed behind him and Carla and Alonzo were left alone to the silence of no music, no coworkers, no party. They got right to work on their volunteered task. Carla put the perishables in the refrigerator and the non-perishables in the cupboard, while Alonzo collected the trash.

Ten minutes later, with the place in good order and all the lights turned off but one, Carla and Alonzo stood by the door ready to leave. And yet…not so ready.

They stared at one another as if there was something they'd forgotten to do. Something seemed unfinished, but what? Carla searched Alonzo's eyes for meaning, but only found more questions.

Out of the awkwardness, Alonzo made a humorous recollection of earlier evening, "Darcy is sure something else, isn't she?"

"Yes," Carla agreed.

Then seriously, he stated, "*You're* something else too, Carla. Something I never imagined."

Her breath quickened. He was coming on to her and she liked it.

"Sorry we only had one dance," he said.

She nodded.

"You look great in that dress," he said.

"It…it's just a dress," Carla tried to downplay its sexuality.

But Alonzo kept admiring her and the dress as if there were no downplay to be had.

She'd bought the dress at the Minneapolis Marshall Field's Store a year ago, and despite it having been on sale she'd never paid as much for any other item of clothing in her whole life as she had for this one. Though she'd beaten herself up many times over the extravagancy, tonight it seemed to come into its full worth.

While Alonzo studied her appearance, Carla studied his. His hands clasped her waist. And she couldn't keep her fingers out of his hair. He and she were definitely headed somewhere. To wherever that might be, Carla felt ready to go anywhere Alonzo led her.

And he knew it.

He reached behind her and clicked off the last light switch to the lunchroom. The befallen darkness made it seem like the whole world suddenly disappeared, except for the two of them now wrapped in each other's arms. They kissed hurriedly at first, as if they'd been tortured by the wait. Then slower, deeper, longer.

Clinging to each other, they found their way across the room to the leather sofa.

It was eleven-thirty when Carla got home. Alonzo had offered to drive her, but she'd told him she was fine. Nevertheless, he followed her in his car just to be sure. She was glad, because she actually did feel a little fuzzy behind the wheel and found her driving less competent than she'd expected. With frequent glances in her rear-view mirror, it'd been a comfort knowing Alonzo was there.

When she pulled into the driveway beside her house, Alonzo, from the street, flicked his car lights twice and drove on.

Carla got out of her car and went up the steps onto the back porch. The moonlight shining softly upon the glider swing was like an invitation for her to sit a while.

She loved that swing. She could spend time alone in it and feel as if she were sharing a special part of her inner self with it that she could never seem to share with any person. Well, she and the swing certainly had a secret now, that was for sure.

Carla kept the swing in a gentle motion. She shivered as the cool night air of May seeped through her light jacket. Despite the chill, the air contained the sweet scent of spring. She took a deep breath, like a hopeful drug to still her conscience. It didn't quite do the trick, for in the silence at the end of her evening her mind was spinning with a wild mixture of unfamiliar emotions. She moaned with frustration, and the swing creaked as if in sympathy.

After a while Carla went inside, through the kitchen, through the living room and up the stairs. After a hot shower that helped her feel cleaner and calmer, she slipped into her nightshirt.

When she crawled into bed next to her husband, she was glad to find him sleeping soundly. Although Keith's lying there breathing so evenly and peacefully gave her a sense of relief in one way, it seemed to worsen her guilt in another. She'd had no reason to cheat on him. He was a good guy. She loved him with all her heart. How could she have let herself be with another man tonight?

The soothing effect of Carla's shower soon faded and her mind was again spinning rampantly. Restless as she was, she was afraid to move for fear of waking Keith. She didn't need Keith to be awake right now. Morning would come soon enough. She drew herself into a fetal position and stared into the silent dark, dreading tomorrow.

CHAPTER 2

Carla awakened to the feel of an arm coming around her and for a scary moment thought it was Alonzo. But it was Keith, thank goodness. As he snuggled against her she tried thinking of him as a precious gift to right her wrong, like everything would be okay now because last night had only been a bad dream.

"'Mornin', beautiful," he said in an intimate, early-morning whisper.

"'Mornin'," she murmured through a yawn and rolled over to him.

He was giving her one of his charismatic grins. "Missed you last night. So tell me what happened at the Milo Printing event."

Oh, the guilt that question brought to Carla. But she answered it from the only direction in which Keith could possibly be coming from. "The company's expanding and we're getting raises."

"Wow. That's great. But ain't that the way," he joked, backing off the bed into the flood of sunshine coming through the east windows, "how some earn extra money through raises while some of us only get it by working six days a week."

Actually Keith always took it well, having to work an occasional Saturday. He liked his job and never tired of it. Although complaints were useless anyway when your boss was your father-in-law.

Carla watched him move about the room. Lean and fit, warm brown eyes, sandy hair, and super good-natured, he wore his white painter clothes with the appeal of a military uniform. She loved watching him. She loved her life with him. She loved him.

He stepped into the adjoining bathroom for a moment, then back out. He took his watch off the dresser, checked the time, and fastened it on his wrist.

"I'll tell you more about it later," Carla said. "Right now I want to know how Jessie did last night."

"She was terrific!" Keith raved of their thirteen-year old daughter who'd had a leading part in her school play. "Sure wish you could've seen her."

"Me too."

When two months ago Jessie had first brought home the news of her doing this, Carla cheered her on. And the day when Jessie came home from her first rehearsal with a bad case of the jitters that had her wanting to quit, Carla gave her the encouragement and self-confidence to stick with it. Carla had been her best supporter all along, until just a few days ago when Milo's mandatory event turned up on the same night as the play.

In her quiet, amiable way Jessie had found no problem with that. Just as Keith hadn't. Ironically, neither of those two realized that their easy-going demeanors could lay just as much of a guilt trip on Carla as their protests would have. And now, for being a person who was so easily burdened with guilt, there were *two* things from last night for her to deeply regret. Missing the play and…

"She was a knockout," Keith continued about Jessie's performance. "She said her lines like a pro and projected them with all the right emotions. Afterwards she, Ryan, your parents and I went out for malts. Kinda thought you'd get home ahead of us, but evidently your dinner meeting ran later than you expected."

"It did," Carla said, expressing her own surprise over it.

"I would have waited up for you, but with this early job today—"

"It's okay." Carla's eyes fell shut, longing for more sleep, more escape.

"So what time *did* you get home?" Keith asked.

Before she could answer, he was on the bed again, cozying up to her with a series of kisses. Luckily he was more interested in a little smooching than a timetable, and thus she got out of answering his question. Despite being wiped out, sad, and hung over, she responded affectionately to him, hopefully hiding her anxiety.

Keith was a good lover. He was passionate, sexy, sincere, and he always made Carla feel ultra special, ultra desirable. Any woman would want him. *She* wanted him. She wasn't throwing him over for Alonzo by any means. That was not what last night was about. She had absolutely no idea *what* last night had been about.

"Damn your father for being a workaholic," Keith sputtered dramatically, forcing himself away from Carla and the bed. He sighed with the frustration of being torn between two loves...his wife and his job.

Carla teasingly reminded him, "But you knew that about him when you first started working for him twenty some years ago."

"Yeah, I did. Wednesdays...Saturdays...Sundays...one day's same as the next to Nathan when it comes to his work. Start painting a house and you gotta stick with it till it's finished, no matter what."

"Customers love him for that," Carla said.

"Don't we all," Keith laughed. He gave her one more good-bye kiss, tagged with, "To be continued tonight."

"Tonight," she agreed.

As soon as he left the room, tears flooded Carla's eyes. There was no way she was going to fall back to sleep now, no matter how hard she tried. She was in for a day of grueling self-reproach and that was that.

She lay there feeling sick. Sick from last night's drinking, since she wasn't a drinker to begin with. Sick from having had sex with Alonzo. Sick with the fear of how she was going to get through this day and the next day and the day after that.

First and foremost she would have to protect Keith from getting hurt. He didn't deserve to be hurt. He didn't deserve a wife who cheated on him. *Oh, God,* she agonized, *what have I done?*

"Mom...?"

Carla wiped her eyes beneath the blanket before peering out at Jessie standing in the bedroom doorway. "Hi, honey. Dad said you were really great last night."

The dark-haired girl, tomboyishly cute in jeans and a Twins sweatshirt, radiated a mixture of apprehension and urgency. "Sorry to bother you, Mom. Dad said you were sleeping in. But do you know where my new green running shoes are?"

The word green sent a wave of nausea through Carla. "Uh...I think beside the rocker in the living room."

"Oh. Yeah. Thanks." Jessie wheeled around and left.

It was a struggle for Carla to get out of bed. Her head ached and her stomach was threatening to throw up. She wondered what was good for a hangover? She didn't know, had never needed to know before now.

Probably coffee for starters. Yes, lots of coffee. And aspirin. And then she would have to get on with things like nothing happened, because nothing did.

Nothing. However when she caught her reflection in the dresser mirror, she was stricken with more guilt than ever. *Who is that woman and what in heaven's name has she done? I don't know her, she's not me. I would never do what she did last night. I'm not a bad person. I'm not. She is, but I'm not.*

Carla continued toward the bathroom, one hand holding her stomach, the other holding her head. The cool hardwood floor beneath her bare feet aided her awakening, and the sun splashing into the room promised some cheer and hope.

By mid morning Carla was feeling better, at least physically. Dressed in her favorite red sweater and faded jeans helped. She made some toast to go with her fourth mug of coffee, and it set well.

Jessie, wearing those ghastly pea-green shoes of hers, was eating a bowl of cereal at the kitchen table. She, as well as Keith, needed protection from getting hurt. Carla studied Jessie, sensing that protecting her daughter was going to be an even more delicate task than protecting her husband.

Attempting more pleasantry, Carla pulled a kitchen curtain aside, saying, "What a beautiful morning, huh? Just look at that sun out there."

Jessie laughed. "It's been out there for hours, Mom, and you're only just now noticing it?"

Guilty. "I admit I started out slow this morning, but I'm coming around."

"How was your dinner meeting last night?"

"Business is good, Milo is moving to a bigger building, and we're getting raises."

"Great."

Guilty. "It shouldn't have been mandatory. I shouldn't have had to miss your play."

"No big deal." Jessie wiped her mouth on her sweatshirt sleeve and took her empty bowl to the sink. "Paul and his brother Mickey are on their way over. We're taking the bike trail all the way out to Greggor's Farm to go horseback riding. You already gave me permission, remember? And Dad gave me money."

"So we did," Carla recalled with a touch of motherly regret. "You will be careful, won't you?"

"No," Jessie said, with her big brown eyes widening. "I'm going to go through red lights with my bike, ride down devil's hill without braking, and pull my horse's tail to make him rear up."

"That's my girl," Carla laughed and went to give her a hug. "Honey, I really am sorry I missed your play last night. Dad said you were great."

"Ryan said I was horrible," Jessie stated her brother's opinion.

Though nineteen-year old Ryan had moved out of the house six months ago and into a small apartment of his own, he still took part in many family events. And though he criticized Jessie on a regular basis, it was understandably done in the teasing manner of sibling love.

"He was razzing you," Carla said knowingly. "I grew up with a brother, too, you know. Though Uncle Mike was a couple years younger than me, he could razz me to tears."

Jessie giggled. Brother grievances were something the two of them fondly shared and compared.

When Jessie took a bottle of water out of the refrigerator and came to a puzzled standstill in the middle of the kitchen, Carla read the question and gave the answer. "Your gray jacket...last I saw it, it was out on the porch swing."

Jessie rolled her eyes and smiled. "Thanks, Mom. You're spooky. Hey—Paul and Mickey just rode up. I'll be careful, really. See ya later."

The screen door banged shut with a sharpness that jolted Carla's mind back to her mistake. She stood alone and hurting. Guilty as she felt in the company of her family, she felt it even worse being alone. She wished Keith wasn't working. She wished Jessie hadn't gone off with friends. She wished Ryan still lived at home, and if he did she would likely be making him a batch of his favorite Saturday-morning pancakes right now.

Carla poured herself more coffee. And while she was wishing things, she wished that last night had never happened. But it had.

Keith didn't mind working a Saturday now and then. Heck, he liked painting houses. Most of the time it actually felt more like a hobby than a job. And working with Carla's dad, Nathan, was definitely more of a pleasure than a hindrance. Nathan, a man of pride and devotion and damn good work, had maintained a successful painting business in and around Tag Lake for over thirty years, and Keith was glad to be a part of that. This spring the weather had warmed up exceptionally early, allowing them a welcomed head start on their outdoor season.

Keith had been a cocky twenty-two-year old looking for a good-paying, easy job when he'd hooked up with Nathan years ago. Nathan had just lost his partner when Keith came along as an eager replacement. Nathan took him on, promising that the money would be good but the work hard. Right off Keith didn't believe painting could be hard, but he soon learned otherwise. Beyond the pleasantry of brush stroking were ladders and scaffolds to deal with, nasty preparation work, required perfection, and time limits pushing into overtime. But more than anything, Keith learned about the rewards in doing a good job, especially in your home town where you could drive around boasting, *hey, I painted that house, that building, that mile-long fence.*

Not long after Keith started working for Nathan, he was invited to his house for dinner. It was then and there that he met the boss's daughter, Carla, and his fanciful bachelorhood came to an end. But he loved every minute of his new life, falling in love, committing to marriage, buying an old fixer-upper house, having kids. He adored his in-laws and continued to work for Nathan. They did outside paint jobs in the summer and inside ones in the winter. Life was great for him in all respects.

The house he and Nathan would finish today was the Richardson's house. It was an eighty-eight year old relic at the edge of Tag Lake's business district. A two-story structure with intricate details and a big front porch. For three generations the Richardsons traditionally cared for its original wood siding with periodic paint jobs. This was the forth time Nathan had been hired to paint it over the years, and it was Keith's second time working on it with him. The color changed this time from white to medium gray with green trim, a good choice that had it looking better than ever and far younger than its actual age.

"What's up?" Keith asked when he found Nathan staring at him.

Nathan was studying him from his ladder perch just over a ways. "You got this…I don't know, this *look* on your face."

Nathan did well with ladders, for being almost seventy. He did everything quite well for being almost seventy. In fact, you could not convince Nathan that he *was* almost seventy. Handsome, silver-haired, muscle-toned and high-spirited, he was invincibly young.

Keith grinned. "A look? You're noticing that I have a look? You're suppose to be watching what you're painting, not how I look."

"I can paint a house and keep an eye on you at the same time."

Keith laughed. "Damn, you're good! But you don't need to keep an eye on me, Nathan. I'm a good painter and a good son-in-law, whether you're watching me or not."

"I know."

"You're not by any chance planning to sucker me into working Sunday too, are you?"

"Nope. Can't work tomorrow myself, even if we don't finish here, though I know that we will. Got a date tonight, might be up late."

"Whoa, does your wife know about this?" Keith pretended to be concerned.

"Sure, Alice supports it. 'Long as my date's with her."

"There's always a catch, isn't there."

"Yeah," Nathan happily admitted. "How about you and Carla? You guys have a date for tonight?"

"Yeah. Sort of. Probably."

Nathan moaned. "That sounds exciting."

"We'll probably have dinner, cuddle on the couch, and watch a video."

"Ahh...and we all know where that leads."

"Nathan, *please*...this is your daughter we're talking about."

"Carla, yeah," Nathan said with heartfelt affection. But then his tone hardened with reference to last night. "Y'know, I just don't get what was so important about her job that she had to choose it over Jessie's play?"

"Big news. Milo Printing is expanding. And my wife's getting a raise. *A raise*, Nathan."

Nathan got the dig. "But is Carla's job as much fun as yours?"

"Yeah, yeah, I know..." Keith agreed sarcastically, "money isn't everything. Especially when you work for a relative."

"Count your blessings."

"Anyway," Keith said, "we didn't get much of a chance to talk yet, but she's going to give me the details tonight. I do know she does feel bad for having missed Jessie's play."

"Jessie was good," Nathan reminisced.

"Yeah," Keith laughed. "She sure belted it out, didn't she?"

"*Gimme the money or I'll kick your teeth in!*" Nathan mimicked one of her lines.

"Hellova thief," Keith said.

"Was nice being with Ryan too. He's a good kid. Seems to be doing well on his own."

"He is."

"Respectable job, auto mechanic."

"Yes, it is."

"As good as a house painter."

"But better pay."

"Y'know, Keith..." Nathan said with a sincerity that caused his eyes to glimmer, "I'm sure glad I didn't retire a year ago when I was contemplating it. I've decided that I just may work till I'm ninety"

Keith grinned. "I can just see you still bossing me around at that age, shaking your cane and yelling orders at me in a feeble voice."

"I'll have promoted you to boss by then," Nathan promised, "and you can boss *me* around. How's that?"

"Gee thanks. But can anyone really boss a ninety-year old around?"

"I'm lucky to have you, kid. As a worker and as a son-in-law. I'm happy, y'know…just real happy." Nathan always displayed his love for life so passionately that one could never underestimate it.

"You're sure in some kind of mood today, aren't you," Keith concluded.

"Of course. The sun is shining, I'm alive and kicking, and I have a date with a beautiful woman tonight. Hallelujah!"

Keith nodded, feeling remarkably happy himself.

CHAPTER 3

Carla was curled up in a living room chair that afternoon, absorbed in a home-decorating magazine, when the front doorbell rang and startled her out of the nice escape she'd finally found. She unfolded herself and went to answer it as it rang out again and again and again. Whatever this was about, it couldn't be good.

It was Darcy. Though it was common for her to occasionally stop by unexpectedly, she'd never rung the doorbell four times in a row and she'd never had the look on her face that she did now.

Carla stood aghast in the open doorway. "Darcy—what's wrong?"

"*You're* asking *me* what's wrong?" Darcy marched past her into the living room.

It was easy to tell that Darcy was here for a specific reason. Though Carla had no idea what that might be, it made her cringe.

Ahead of Carla, Darcy plopped into an easy chair, crossed her arms, and gave a huff. Carla retook her original chair, bracing herself for the unimaginable.

"You certainly made a night of it, didn't you!" Darcy then blurted, as if they were preplanned words she could no longer hold back.

Surely she couldn't be referring to Alonzo. It sounded like it, but no, there was no way she could know about…

"Right?" Darcy dared Carla to admit.

Carla took a deep breath. "I shouldn't have drank, right, but I'm fine now. You needn't be worried about me if that's what you—"

"Worried? Bullshit!" Darcy socked her fist into the arm of her chair. Then glancing about, she verified, "We're alone here, aren't we?"

"Keith's working and Jessie's out. Yes, we're alone, you and me. Why are you jumping on me like this, Darcy?"

"Good word, *jumping*." Darcy's eyes grew larger and darker by the minute. "But I never would've imagined you and Alonzo doing it."

"Darcy!" Carla gasped.

Darcy popped out of her chair. "Got a cigarette?"

"You know I don't smoke, and neither do you."

"You don't drink either, right?"

"It was Marty's specials. He kept—"

"Bullshit! Sure you had more drinks than a beginner ought to, but you weren't drunk. You knew exactly what you were doing, going after Alonzo, staying after the party with him."

Darcy knew, *but how*? It was as if Carla's dark, dirty secret had been publicized to the world. She got to her feet, facing her friend directly, hoping to clarify. "It's not what you think. I just—"

"You didn't screw him?"

"It was a mistake, Darcy. All a mistake. How…how did you even know about it? You left the party earlier and—"

"I got just about home and realized I'd left my wallet on a lunchroom table. I'd taken it out of my purse to show Tom a picture of my cat, then Milo started to give his talk and I forgot to put it away. I drove back to get it, pulled into the back lot and—"

Carld held up a stop hand. She didn't want to hear any more.

Darcy nevertheless continued, "The place was dark, pitch black when I returned. Because, of course, the party was over and everyone went home, right? Except there were two cars in the parking lot. Gosh…were they yours and Alonzo's? Gosh…yes. And so then where were you guys? Well, I could only figure that you were inside the dark lunchroom of Milo Printing doing God only knows what. Well, actually, I guess both God and I did know."

Carla hung her head. She loved Darcy, but there had always been this fine line between trusting and not trusting her. Carla knew she was on the negative side of that line right now. There was something cruel in Darcy's intentions.

"Needless to say," Darcy went on, "I didn't attempt to go inside the building for my wallet. I didn't want to interrupt anything. Anyway, when I got home there was a message on my answering machine from Milo. He'd found my wallet after I'd left and wanted me to know he put it in my desk drawer."

"A mistake," Carla made an another attempt to justify the happening.

"I never knew you had a thing for Alonzo," Darcy said.

"I didn't…don't…it was the drinks, Darcy, I swear. My evening started out with this horrible guilt I had of having to miss Jessie's school play. I…I guess I turned to a few drinks in hopes of easing that."

"And the drinks weren't enough? You had to turn to Alonzo besides?"

Carla exhausted a heavy sigh. "I didn't turn to Alonzo. I…you don't understand. Oh, I wish I *did* have a cigarette."

"Or another drink? Or another shot at Alonzo?"

"Stop it!" Carla said. "Why are you doing this to me? So what if I did do what I did? Can't you see, as my best friend, that I'm feeling pretty rotten over it and could use a little understanding from you right now?"

Darcy laughed and gave a shrug. "Sure, honey, you're right. You're a happily-married woman with a great husband, kids, house, life. Why shouldn't I be more understanding when you decide to shack up with a coworker?"

"That's not how it was."

"You had it all. You didn't have to take him."

"I didn't take him."

"You *took* him," Darcy insisted. "The only guy I've ever seriously been interested in since my divorce."

Carla blinked her eyes in dismay. "You…?"

Darcy's moment of silence exposed a deluge of pain and suffering. It seemed she was feeling even worse than Carla was over what happened.

"I'm sorry," Carla said, with her guilt intensifying.

"There aren't many good ones out there," Darcy stated, as if she'd personally taken a census. "I've been pretty disillusioned about men since Bill. But when Alonzo came along I thought maybe if I just took my time and played my cards right…" Darcy paused, recapturing her wrath. "Anyway, before I got a decent chance with him, you went and wrecked it all. Thank you, Carla. *Thank you very much.* You just have to have it all, don't you? Well, I guess that's what it means when they say blondes have more fun."

"A mistake…" Carla pleaded in a small, but desperate, voice.

"You got that right," Darcy agreed, then started for the door.

Carla hurried after her. "I didn't know! Darcy, wait! Don't leave like this! You know I'd never hurt you on purpose. You know I'd never do what I did last night if I hadn't been under the influence."

Darcy stopped at the door and refaced her. "I'm really, really disappointed in you, blondie…you know? You make me sick. The only time I ever want to see you again, and I don't even want to then but it'll be necessary, is at work."

"Darcy, please…I'm feeling so bad over this that…you…you've got to understand and—"

"No, no, dear…I think the only one who needs to understand now is Keith. You *are* going to tell him, aren't you? I mean, you guys supposedly have the perfectly honest marriage, don't you?"

Carla felt as if the blood were being drained out of her, and she'd never felt so close to fainting. "Keith doesn't need to know. I would never hurt him like that."

Darcy sneered like a she-devil from hell. "You mean, like what he doesn't know won't hurt him? Is that what you mean? Well, maybe I care about Keith more than I care about you right now. And maybe I think he should know the truth. If you don't tell him, Carla, I will."

This wasn't happening. Occasional friction between the women, yes, but never anything as threatening as this. "Don't tell him. Please. Please don't, Darcy. Alonzo means nothing to me. Last night meant nothing to me. I don't think he knows that you have feelings for him, but you could tell him. Why don't you just tell him how you feel about him. Go for him. He's all yours."

Darcy's eyes narrowed as she pointed a finger in Carla's face. "You tell your husband about this or I will."

"No, Darcy, come on…you know me and—"

"Not anymore do I know you. Good-bye, Carla. I'll give Keith a call sometime next week…just to ask how he is. I mean, you know, I like Keith."

Jessie stood in the kitchen, just around the corner from the living room. She'd returned home, came in the back way and grabbed some cookies to take back outside for Paul, Mickey and herself. While she was there, the voices of her mom and Darcy caught her attention and she couldn't help eavesdropping. It turned out being an earful she wished she hadn't heard.

When she went back out onto the porch, the guys noticed the drop in her mood.

"What happened in there?" Paul asked. Despite his concern, he was eager for the cookie she gave him.

Looking equally as concerned, Mickey also accepted a cookie from her.

Standing at the railing, Jessie broke her own cookie into pieces and tossed them into the yard for the birds.

"What's wrong?" Paul asked her again.

"Nothing," she said.

"Doesn't sound like nothing."

"Nothing," she repeated.

"So you want to bike the parkway path next?" Paul suggested.

Jessie shook her head. "I'm done biking for today. Except, I do need to bike over to Ryan's. I need to talk to my brother."

She caught Paul and Mickey exchanging puzzled looks, realizing she was letting them down like some emotional, drippy girl. But she couldn't help it that her eyes were misty and her voice trembled.

"Okay," Paul allowed her. "See you later."

"Later," Jessie said.

"Later," Mickey said, following Paul off the porch.

The guys left on their bikes, and in another minute Jessie was mounting her own. Rage was swelling so fast within her she felt as if any moment she might explode. She was glad Ryan lived no farther away than three miles. As it was, she wasn't going to be able to get there fast enough.

Ryan's apartment was in a small complex with no garages. She always knew he was home when she saw his beater car parked in the lot. It sat there now, giving Jessie a welcomed sense of relief.

She locked her bike to the front entrance railing. The conversation between her mother and Darcy was pounding in her head like a rock song with no melody, only drums. Though she couldn't accept what she'd overheard back at the house as real, it certainly wasn't disappearing like it was nothing.

The building was non-secure, thus Jessie let herself in and climbed the inner stairs to third floor. She knocked on Ryan's apartment door. He opened it with a surprised look on his face.

While Jessie's features favored her dad's, Ryan's favored Carla's. Blonde, blue-eyed, as cute as any girl's desirable hunk, Ryan smiled affectionately at his kid sister. "Hey…you look like you seen a ghost. Or a mouse…or a bug…or…"

Jessie stormed on in past him. She was on a mission too important to joke about.

"What's up?" Ryan asked, taking her more seriously.

"Did I say anything was?" Now that Jessie was there, she wasn't all together sure she was ready to talk about this. Maybe saying it out loud to him would make it hurt all the more.

"Come on, spill it," he urged her.

Jessie sat down on the dilapidated couch. "You need new furniture in here."

"That's *my* problem, now tell me yours."

"It's Mom."

"Mom?"

"You're not going to believe this, Ryan."

"More like I'm not going to hear it," he said impatiently. "Why don't you just say what it is you came here to tell me?"

Jessie wrung her hands together on her knees and stared at the floor. This was hard, really hard. But Ryan was older and wiser and would undoubtedly know what to do. It was great, having a big brother to depend on. She gave him a hopeful look. "Mom's having an affair."

Ryan had no smart comeback to that.

"Mom is having an affair," Jessie repeated.

Ryan's face filled with horror. "Where'd you get this idea?"

"Straight from her. I accidentally overheard her and Darcy talking in our living room. At the company party she went to last night…she…Mom…made it with some guy she works with."

Ryan slowly lowered himself beside Jessie on the couch. "No…come on, no…" he murmured, more to himself than to her.

She put her hand on his arm. "What are we going to do, Ryan?"

"What do you mean what are we going to do? There's nothing we can do. What could you even imagine that we could do?"

"I don't know. Something. We have to do something."

When Ryan put a brotherly arm around her, that was all it took for Jessie to burst into tears. "Don't worry," was all he could tell her, with his own eyes glimmering.

After a few quiet minutes, Ryan got up and started for the kitchen. "I was in the midst of doing dishes when you came. Guess I'll finish them."

"Dishes?" Jessie scowled, following him. "How can you think of doing dishes at a time like this?"

Ryan didn't answer but rather only plunged his hands into the sudsy water.

After staring disappointedly at him for a few minutes, Jessie grabbed a dishtowel and began to dry to his washing. She supposed it was better than sitting there crying.

Eventually she lightened up enough to comment, "You'll make a good husband for some girl some day."

He laughed and turned it back on her. "And you just might make a good wife for some guy some day."

Jessie punched him in the arm. "Yuk!"

They laughed together briefly. But when they finished the dishes they became ultra serious again, sitting on stools at the kitchen counter, discussing their parents like a couple of parents discussing their kids.

"What about Dad?" Jessie worried most about him. "Darcy threatened to tell him about last night if Mom doesn't."

"Mom will," Ryan said with more confidence than Jessie could warrant. "She's honest."

There was no way Jessie could connect honesty to adultery. She folded her arms across her chest and moaned.

"There's nothing you and I can do about this," Ryan tried to assure her. "We just have to wait and see."

"Like until they get divorced?"

"They won't get divorced."

"How do you know that?" Jessie argued. "After what happened? After Dad finds out?"

"Because," Ryan said softly, "Mom and Dad are Mom and Dad. And we just have to trust them to work it out, okay?"

Jessie couldn't agree with that. Right now she had little trust in anyone or anything.

CHAPTER 4

Darcy's visit slammed Carla's day from bad to worse. Now, on top of everything else from last night, their friendship was ruined. Yet, Carla now had to wonder how shallow had their friendship actually been to begin with? Or did she truly deserve as much from Darcy? Deserve...there was a word to be reckoned with. Carla didn't feel she deserved getting so lost from herself last night. If only Marty hadn't pushed those tasty drinks onto her. More so, if Jessie's play had only been on a different night when she could've gone she wouldn't have had the guilt of missing it, which started her drinking at Milo's in the first place.

And then there was Alonzo, the biggest and most unexpected source of the problem. This was ultimately his fault for coming onto her the way he did. His asking her to dance, his seductive looks and words, and then his turning out that last lunchroom light. Who would have thought him to behave that way? Or her to respond as she did? It was a company event. She should have been safe there from such a thing happening. She might have been safe had she not been drinking. She might not have had so many drinks, had Marty not kept coddling her with them. She might not have ever started drinking had she not been so upset over missing Jessie's play.

"Shit!" Carla shouted out of her frustration. Recognizing that she only had herself to blame for all of this didn't make her feel any better. What happened, happened. She couldn't go backwards, only forward. It wouldn't be easy, keeping this from Keith, but it would surely be easier than telling him. It was a secret worth keeping. He would never know about it from her, and surely Darcy wasn't serious about telling him.

It took everything Carla had to work up the nerve to lift the kitchen phone and dial a familiar number. When her mother answered, Carla felt choked up.

"Hello? Is anyone there?" the voice on the line asked.

"Mom…hi," Carla said.

"What's wrong?"

It was hard to fool your mother, but Carla cleared her throat and tried. "Just called to say hi and ask what you're doing."

The voice laughed softly. "You and I…we've been Saturday widows for three weeks in a row now, haven't we. What do you think…should we make protest signs or go shopping?"

Carla smiled sadly. "Guess I'll pass on both today."

"Oh…really?"

"Just feel like having a little phone chat, that's all."

"Sure. Okay. We can chat. I need a break from my crocheting, and I really don't have anything to shop for. But…you sure everything's okay, dear?"

"Everything's fine," Carla insisted, forcing some strength into her voice. "How are things for you?"

"I'm fine. Your father and I have a date tonight."

Carla laughed with an undertone of jealousy. Until last night her own marriage had been as sweet and easy.

From there the conversation between the two women rambled over an assortment of topics that lasted nearly a half-hour. But when it ended, and Carla hung up finding it hadn't been all she'd hoped it to be, she broke down into a hard cry.

She was glad when five o'clock came and she could start supper. She desperately needed something routinely normal to do. She wasn't hungry, even though she hadn't eaten all day except for toast in the morning. But she had a husband who would soon be home and starving, and a growing teenager who…

The back screen door banged, announcing Jessie's arrival.

Carla turned away from the Hamburger Helper she was tending to on the stove, finding a forlorn look on her daughter's face. "Did you fall off the horse?"

"No," Jessie answered.

"Bike?"

"I'm fine."

Carla stopped Jessie from walking straight on through the kitchen. "Hey, wait a minute."

"Fine," Jessie repeated in a tone that said otherwise.

Carla studied her daughter, seeing a problem but not its origin. Jessie was a cheerful child; where was this gloomy spirit suddenly coming from? "Wann'a talk about it?" she offered.

"Talk about what?" Jessie responded nervously, seeming ultra anxious to leave the kitchen.

"You're upset about something."

"No," Jessie snapped, "I'm not."

"Oh," Carla said. And as soon as she let up on the pressure, Jessie continued out of there and went thundering upstairs.

When Keith got home, he came up behind Carla at the stove and gave her a bear hug. She knew from the way his body pressed into hers that he was going to want to make love tonight. It scared her, threatened her. She was going to have to be a good actress, having sex with him while hiding the fact that last night she'd been with another man.

"About last night..." Carla was first to open a conversation during supper.

Jessie choked on something, coughed a couple times, then gulped a drink of milk.

Keith flashed her a look. "You okay?"

Jessie nodded.

"About Milo's expanding," Carla continued, "John bought the old Gantly building and we've just landed a huge contract from Tomlin's."

"Plus you're all getting raises!" Keith cheered. "Sounds like last night's mandatory event had its significance."

His enthusiasm was great. She wished Jessie shared in it. It wasn't like her to be moody. Carla could only think that maybe her not being at the play last night bothered Jessie more than she was actually letting on.

Just as Carla was about to extend another apology for her absence last night, Jessie pushed herself back from the table, saying, "Excuse me...I'm not hungry...I've got homework to do."

"She hates me," Carla concluded to Keith when they were alone.

"Naw..." he said, "I think it's more that she hates homework."

Carla managed a slight smile. "Yeah, maybe."

Later the two of them sat snuggled together on the couch, watching the Jim Carey DVD Keith had picked up on his way home from work. With one arm holding her, his free hand made repeated visits to the bowl of M & M's on the other side of him.

"Mmm..." he sighed, "how good is this, huh?"

Carla tilted her face toward his. "Me? Or the M & M's? Or Jim Carey?"

He laughed, deliberately not answering. He was out of his painter clothes now and into a pair of old jeans and a navy tee shirt. He looked boyish and relaxed. So oblivious of any harm.

"I'm sorry about last night," Carla offered, as if she were almost ready to give herself away.

"I can see now how important it was for Milo to have his group there, so just drop the guilt, okay, honey?"

"But if Milo could've just—"

Keith stopped her words by kissing her, and Carla willingly fell captive.

When they broke from their little romantic interlude, they noticed Jessie standing in the doorway of the low-lighted living room. She looked strange, sad, lost.

"Hey, Jess…" Keith acknowledged her. "Come watch this movie with us."

Embarrassed over having walked in on her parents kissing, she lowered her eyes and spoke in a stammer, "Saw it…no, thanks…I…I've got stuff to do."

"Still doing homework?" Carla asked.

"No. Finished. Just…stuff…upstairs…in my room. I just came down for some cookies."

Keith laughed. "Can't do stuff without cookies."

Jessie proceeded to the kitchen. The cookie jar cover rattled. She came back through the hallway, past the living room door, said good night, and scurried back upstairs.

"She didn't eat much supper," Carla reasoned.

"Mmm…" Keith murmured, turning his attention back on his wife, "where were we?"

Kissing had been nice, but when his hands began claiming more of her, Carla realized she couldn't do this. Not yet, not tonight. Much to Keith's astonishment, she pushed him away.

"What's wrong?" he asked.

"Nothing. I mean…yeah, something…I'm…I'm just a little over tired, I guess. Would you mind…?"

Keith settled back on his side of the couch, trying to make like it was okay. "Guess you prefer Jim Carey to me right now."

Despite his disappointment, Keith made her laugh. And he laughed too. And it seemed they were okay again. For now.

"I'm sorry," she still needed to say.

"Me too." Keith gave her a tender look as he pushed play on the remote.

"Darcy came over this afternoon," Carla also felt the need to tell him, in spite of the movie coming into play again.

"Like you two don't see enough of each other at work all week, not to mention last night?"

"We...Darcy and me...we had a fight."

"Fight?" Keith was first amused, then sympathetic. His look left the movie for Carla. "You guys are best friends. What happened?"

"Just...girl stuff. Sometimes, I don't know, I think maybe she and I are too close. Sometimes that sort of relationship sets you up for getting too touchy over the slightest things."

"Mmm, sorry. Maybe it'll all be better Monday when you see each other at work."

Carla slid back closer to Keith, soothed by his easy nature. "I love you."

He smiled. "I know. I love you too."

Their concentration was barely back into the movie plot when the phone rang. Keith pushed pause on the remote and went out to the kitchen to catch it.

Carla waited on the couch. She was nervous, as in afraid the phone call might be Darcy calling to inform Keith about his unfaithful wife. Darcy had threatened to tell him, but no, she couldn't have meant it. Couldn't. Keith must never know. There was no reason for him to know. Darcy had to respect that. Had to.

"Who was it?" Carla was quick to ask on his return.

Laughing, he rejoined her on the couch. "Ryan. He was just wondering if we were okay."

"If we were okay?"

"Yeah. I told him we were. And when I asked him why, he said he just more or less felt like calling to say hi."

"I think he misses living here," Carla justified.

"I know I sure would," Keith said. He put his arm around Carla, pushed play on the remote, and Jim Carey again won their attention.

They seemed okay, her parents, Jessie thought, having seen the way the two of them were together on the couch, watching a movie of all things. They didn't act like a couple on the brink of divorce. Although, maybe, probably, her dad didn't even know yet that there was a problem, another man.

Jessie wished that she herself didn't know. It would be so much better not knowing. She'd lied about having her homework done. She hadn't even started it. Who could concentrate on World War II after just learning that your mother was a slut?

Stretched across her bed with her cell phone, she called Ryan. "It's me."

"Jessie." He was surprised, as though he'd already done his brotherly duty for the day and didn't expect to be needed again so soon.

"This is so hard..." she moaned.

"Just a few minutes ago I called the folks. Talked to Dad. He seemed fine."

"Only because he doesn't know yet. They're watching a movie together, as if nothing was wrong."

"Jessie...oh, Jessie...maybe nothing *is* wrong. Maybe this will never amount to anything more."

"How can you say that?"

"Don't you trust in them? In their twenty-year marriage?"

"I don't know."

"I think we can, little sister. I really think we can."

Jessie and Ryan talked for a while. And afterwards Jessie felt that phoning her brother did her little good. He was taking this all too optimistically, while she was in panicville. Maybe his age made the difference. Maybe when she got a few years older she, too, would have a higher pain tolerance.

She got off the bed, walked across the room and opened the door a crack. She listened, faintly hearing Jim Carey's dialogue, some silly sound effects, and her mother and dad's laughter. She shut the door, leaned against it, looked up at the ceiling, moaned, and rolled her eyes.

CHAPTER 5

Routinely every Sunday at two Carla, Keith, Ryan and Jessie had dinner at Carla's parents' house. Alice adored cooking, never considered it work, and Nathan took pleasure in setting the dining room table. He hand printed place cards that he put out every time just for fun with the titles *Daughter, Son-in-law, Grandson, Granddaughter, Wife,* and *Me*. He changed their placement each week so that no one knew where they were going to sit at the table until they found their card. Since his grandkids especially got a kick out of it when they were little, Nathan kept it going over the years as a tradition.

Carla loved her parents and the times she and Keith and the kids spent with them. Nathan and Alice still lived in the same old house on Maple Street where Carla and her brother Mike grew up. It was a great house, full of love and home improvements and honest simplicity and endearing memories.

She wished Mike didn't live so far away as San Francisco so that he could be at family gatherings more often. She missed him. He was as wonderful as a brother could be. Too wonderful to only see once a year or so, but they kept in touch best as they could.

Carla was ready to go, and while she waited for Keith and Jessie to be ready she went around the house with her watering can, tending her plants.

"You're watering an artificial plant," Jessie informed Carla, as she came into the living room and caught her pouring water onto a plastic ivy.

Carla became aware of it and laughed at herself, but Jessie's reaction was more solemn than amused. In fact Carla had already noticed before now that Jessie was lacking her usual enthusiasm for going to her grandparents'.

"I'm sorry about the other night," Carla thought it was a good time to throw in another apology. "For missing your play. Jessie, I—"

"It's all right," the girl said coolly. "There are things more important than school plays."

"If you're referring to my job, no it's not more important. It was just a requirement that I—"

"I understand what it was," Jessie snapped.

"Okay, I'm ready, let's go!" Keith came downstairs in good spirits, only to find his wife and daughter at odds over something. He stopped in the middle of the room, looking back and forth at the two of them.

"I'll wait in the car," Jessie said and took off.

"What's going on?" Keith asked Carla.

Carla could only figure that her missing the school play mattered much more to Jessie now than it originally had. She put down the watering can and grabbed her purse. "Let's go."

"Ahh, teenagers, huh?" Keith tried making light of it as they headed out to Carla's car.

Jessie sat tight-mouthed and very much to herself in the back seat, as Carla and Keith got into the front, Keith behind the wheel. The three of them rode to Alice and Nathan's in silence.

Ryan was already there when they arrived, sitting on the front porch with Nathan. Keith parked in the driveway behind Ryan's beater.

Nathan greeted his daughter and granddaughter with hugs and gave Keith a hardy slap on the back. Ryan got out of his chair and spoke hellos to his family. Then Alice, a petite woman, with rosy cheeks, bursting smiles, and an apron over her skirt, came out the door to welcome everyone and announce that they were having goulash for dinner.

It was Ryan's absolute favorite meal and it turned the handsome, grownup nineteen-year old into an ecstatic kid. "Oh, great! Thanks, Grandma! Hope there'll be leftovers for me to take home."

Alice shooed her hand at him. "You know I always make plenty!"

As Ryan walked into the house, Jessie walked close at his side whispering to him. For whatever it was about, they both looked troubled. Carla watched them with curious concern. And then she noticed her own mother watching her in the same way.

Everyone went to the dining-room table to locate their individual place cards.

"Hey, I'm head of the table today," Jessie cheered on her first happy note of the day.

"I'm in the corner." Keith laughed as he moved the large floor plant that always crowded that particular space.

Alice brought in the remaining serving bowls of food, and Nathan spoke his usual dinner prayer.

Carla wasn't hungry. She'd had no appetite yesterday or today. When the goulash came around the table to her she took only a small portion, and when the baked beans came she hoped no one noticed that she took none.

But her mother did. "You're not eating?"

"I am," Carla said, adding a biscuit to her plate.

Carla saw Jessie lean toward Ryan and whisper something to him that he obviously didn't like. He gave her a silent scowl, then flashed a nervous look over at Carla as if the matter might be about her.

Alice was equally aware and bold enough to ask, "You two have a secret?"

At the same time as Ryan answered no, Jessie answered yes. Keith and Nathan laughed, but Carla and Alice exchanged looks of motherly concern.

"This is great, Grandma!" Ryan said, ahead of shoveling food into his mouth.

Alice smiled proudly, then told Jessie, "We're having your favorite for dessert, dear."

"Cherry cheesecake!" The girl brightened immensely. "Thanks, Grandma."

"You know what *my* favorite is?" Keith asked of anyone in general. When everyone looked at him, he said, "Just being here like this, that's my favorite."

"Ooooh..." Alice cooed, "how nice."

"Careful," Nathan warned her, "sounds like your son-in-law may be buttering you up for something."

Alice obviously felt no threat. "With or without buttering, Keith knows he has a special way with me."

"You'll never hear any cruel mother-in-law jokes from me," he promised.

"So what's your favorite, Carla?" Nathan asked her.

She stopped playing with her biscuit. Everyone was waiting for her answer. She had to say something. But oh...uh...*what was the question*? Her favorite thing, right. In her mind she was wishing she were home sitting in her swing.

But as a more appropriate answer to the here and now of everyone's waiting on her, she said, "These biscuits, they're my favorite. I wish I could bake them from scratch like you do, Mom."

Alice laughed. "Perhaps it's time I give you my secret recipe."

Carla grinned. "I'm almost forty, yes, Mom, I think I've waited long enough."

"A baby, you're still just a baby," Nathan told her. Then he winked at Alice, suggesting, "Let's make her wait till she's fifty, huh, Mom?"

Carla studied her parents with pure adoration. She wondered if Alice would ever begin to show her age. Sixty-five looked more like fifty-five on her. Glowing face, taunt skin, girlish figure, and only slight traces of gray mingled amidst her brown hair. Her dad, Nathan, wasn't the worst for wear either. Though his hair was totally gray, he had the body and the energy of a much younger man. Good living and exuberant happiness worked well for the couple. She looked at Keith, wanting as much for the two of them.

"You're not eating," Alice again observed of her.

"Yes, I am," Carla insisted, forking up some goulash. "This is so good. I sure can't make it as good as you do."

"That's for sure," Ryan teased her.

"Hey…" Carla laughed.

"Why do you think I left home?" he pushed it further.

"You can't blame Mom's cooking for your leaving home," Jessie razzed him. "We all know it was just to have a place to bring girls."

Ryan gave her a warning look.

Keith played dumb. "I thought it was so you could stay up and watch TV as late as you wanted at night."

"Yeah, *with girls*," Jessie said.

"Well, a man's gotta do what a man's gotta do, right, Ryan?" Nathan reasoned.

Ryan, with a mouthful of goulash, nodded.

"Right, Keith?" Nathan secondly asked him.

Keith shifted on his chair and glanced across the table at Carla. "It's just that sometimes I guess a man just doesn't know exactly what it really is that he's suppose to do."

"Huh?" Nathan gave him a bewildered squint.

"Oh, we women can set you straight any time you boys need straightening," Alice offered. "Right, Carla?"

Carla was feeling personally attacked. Mostly by her guilt and shame. She excused herself from the table and made a quick retreat to the kitchen. The family would wonder about her behavior, but likely more so if she'd stayed.

She opened the back door and stood by it, taking in large needy breaths of fresh air. Her whole world was so different now. Since her mistake. *She* was different now. She was small and fragile and scared, and there seemed to be second meanings to everything everyone said and did. Punishment seemed to be coming at her from every direction. Punishment from people who didn't even know what she'd done.

Just when she finally began to feel calmer and ready to go back to the dining room, Alice came checking on her.

Carla read her mother's unasked question and told her, "I'm okay. I just needed a…a drink of water."

Alice regarded her daughter's lie with a smile. "We've water glasses at the table, dear."

"I know," Carla admitted.

When the two of them returned to the dinner table, Nathan threw out what felt like another attack on Carla. "Keith said your Milo news was good, so how about filling us in on more details from Friday night."

Carla retook her seat. More punishment. She had to take it. "Business is expanding, we're getting a new location, some additional employees, and raises." In her head she prayed for the Milo subject to end right there.

"You hear that?" Keith razzed Nathan. "The word raise? Does that mean anything to you? Does it give you any ideas?"

Before Nathan could attempt to answer, Jessie anxiously disbursed, "Milo's meeting Friday night turned into quite a party."

Carla didn't like Jessie's discriminatory tone and party assessment. Where on earth was she coming from? She could only be referring to the big dinner Milo put on, but somehow it sounded like she was inferring so much more.

Catching Ryan giving Jessie another of his strange shut-up looks made Carla all the more uneasy.

Keith leaned toward her to ask, "You all right?"

Carla nodded yes. Keith settled back in his chair, accepting that, but the look on Alice's face indicated she wasn't buying her daughter's welfare as readily.

🍁 🍁 🍁

It didn't surprise Nathan that after their company had left Alice was bursting to talk about the gathering. She usually *was* full of comments at this point.

She followed him into the living room, saying, "Something's wrong with that family. I just know it."

"Here we go," Nathan said with an amused roll of his eyes and toss of his hands. "Now you're going to start in on how it'd been a nice afternoon *except for*…"

"Don't tell me you didn't notice, because I know you did."

Nathan grinned. "You're a mind reader now?"

"I know your mind very well, yes, thank you. Enough to know that you saw something unordinary about that family, too, today."

"They seemed fine to me," he said. And supposing they didn't, Nathan didn't want to start picking apart something that wasn't their business. "Good food, good company, amen," he added, heading for his chair with the Sunday paper.

Alice settled into another chair, quiet for a time, as though she was absorbed in some very puzzling thoughts. Then suddenly she burst with, "*Guilty.*"

"Huh?" Nathan glanced at her over the top of his reading glasses.

"The word that fits Carla's conduct today. She looked guilty about something."

"Well, she should. She missed Jessie's school play the other night to go to a party, right? It darn well ought'a lay a guilt trip on her. Can't imagine where her head was."

Alice only half agreed. "Yeah…I guess…I mean, she must be feeling really bad over it. That must be her problem. But what about the kids?"

Nathan rustled his newspaper, searching for the sports section.

"Jessie was quiet," Alice analyzed.

"That's bad?" Nathan quipped.

"And Ryan…did you pick up on the looks he was always giving Carla?"

"No."

"Something's going on," Alice insisted.

"Here." Nathan rolled up the comic section of the paper and threw it across the room to her. "You haven't seen these yet."

Alice put the paper aside. She was on a case now that took her entire attention, and she wasn't going to get off it until she solved it. Though she let up on Nathan about it for now, he knew there would be more discussion about Carla's family later.

🍁 🍁 🍁

Carla spent a long time in the bathroom that night. She felt needy of some extra pampering, extra face cream, extra elbow lotion, extensive teeth brushing, and deep soul searching as she stared at herself in the mirror. Mostly, purposely, she was delaying joining Keith in bed.

When she eventually left her little retreat and started into the bedroom, he was in the process of hanging up the nightstand phone. It was ten-thirty, he was already in bed and Carla was getting there. A call this late couldn't be good. Carla came to a stop in the middle of the room.

"It was your dad," Keith told her. The tone of his voice told her not to worry. "He was just checking to see if everything was all right."

As glad as Carla was that the phone call wasn't an emergency, it's purpose didn't make sense since they'd all been together just a few hours ago. She was again feeling attacked. But only by way of her own inner guilt, because no one else but Darcy knew about her cheating. It only *seemed* like they did.

"Anyway," Keith said, "Nathan thought before he turned in he'd just give us a call to soothe his mind…of which Alice apparently had managed to mangle pretty good."

"Doesn't sound like them."

"I told him we were fine. He said okay, good night, and hung up."

Carla became consciously aware that she was still standing there in the middle of the room in her nightgown while Keith was taking in the view with pleasure.

"We should get to sleep," she said, heading for her side of the bed. "Work tomorrow."

Keith turned out the light and rolled toward her. His touch was warm and tender and felt better than Carla knew she deserved.

Not yet, not now, her body language clearly told him. As hurt as he had to be, he gave her a kiss on her cheek and went back to his side of the bed.

"Sorry," Carla offered through the dark distance between them.

Keith's silence seemed like his own form of rejection. And thus Carla, too, was hurt. She longed to be her old self with him. But it was probably going to take more time than two days. She would make it up to him, she would. Just not tonight.

CHAPTER 6

❀

Monday morning terrified Carla even more than Saturday and Sunday had. She didn't want to go to work. How could she ever again? She stayed in bed, eyes closed, hugging her pillow and listening to Keith moving about the bedroom. When he came to shake her shoulder gently for the third time, she made a little moan to let him know that she was at least alive.

"Really, Carla—you're going to be late if you don't get a move on." Keith bent down to give her a good-bye kiss on the forehead.

She opened her eyes partway.

"See you tonight," he said as pleasantly as if nothing were wrong, as if he hadn't again been intimately rejected by her last night.

"Keith…" Carla called to him as he started out of the room, "I love you."

"I know," he said. "Love you too."

As he left, Jessie stepped into the doorway.

Carla knew the look. "What can't you find?"

"History book."

"I thought you said you did all your homework. If you'd have used it to do your homework over the weekend you should know where it is, shouldn't you?" Carla regretted the sharpness she used on Jessie. Softer and slower she added, "I think I saw it on top of the refrigerator. Though I can't imagine why it would be there."

Jessie said thanks, left, and thudded down the stairs.

Carla moaned. Oh, how easy it would be to call in sick to Milo and snuggle back down to sleep. Oh, if she could just hide out for the day from people and places and things of discomfort. But she couldn't allow herself to cave in like that. This was only the beginning of all she was going to have to deal with, and she knew that the only way to deal with it was to deal with it.

Darcy was already busy sorting papers at the front counter when Carla arrived at Milo Printing. The two women exchanged chilly glances. Neither of them spoke.

Carla and Darcy each had their own desk behind the counter, and Carla went to sit at hers. As she fumbled about her desktop objects feeling lost toward beginning any actual task, she glanced at the door to the print shop, wondering if Alonzo had come to work today. But yes, of course, he no doubt did. Men didn't get all rattled, like women did, about inappropriate behavior. They even had different perspectives as to what was and wasn't considered inappropriate. Possibly Alonzo was in there right now boasting to the other guys about his conquest Friday night. But no, on second thought, Carla knew he wasn't that sort of guy. No…Alonzo was the kind of guy who…

Her heart skipped a beat when the shop door opened and Alonzo came into the front office. He looked startled at first, as if he hadn't expected her to be there today. Then his eyes held hard with hers, as if she were a puzzle he couldn't solve.

Darcy, bless her soul, broke the tension by asking him, "Something I can help you with?" Her voice to him lacked its usual flirtatiousness and was instead tinged with scorn.

Alonzo didn't seem to notice Darcy's demeanor one way or the other. Though he answered her, he was still looking at Carla. "I need the order from Logan's Landscaping."

Carla started to rise from her desk, but Darcy already had the document he wanted in her hands. "Here. It came in late Friday afternoon. *Friday*," she added with emphasis.

Alonzo took the paper from her, gave a stiff nod, and went back to the shop.

"Now tell me," Darcy couldn't wait to seek judgement, "do you think he's feeling passion or pissed over Friday night's sex?"

"Stop it!" Carla said.

Darcy smiled wickedly. "Roses on your desk might've been nice."

"Darcy, be quiet."

"Oh, that's right, it's a secret. Alonzo's, yours and mine."

Carla worried that someone would walk in on them. "Please…this isn't easy." As she nervously swiveled her chair she accidentally bumped over the wastebasket, blasted the word *dang*, and bounced it back upright with a thud.

"No, it's not easy," Darcy agreed. "Things are never going to be easy around here again, you know that, Carla?"

Tears were welling in Carla's eyes. Ten minutes at work and she's *crying*. How she wished she were home, or anywhere but here. "You know, I could really use a friend right now instead of harassment."

"You don't know the meaning of friend."

"Darcy, don't turn on me like this."

"I believe you're the one who turned."

"I'm feeling really sick over Friday and—"

John Milo burst through the front door. "'Morning, girls. Happy Monday."

Carla and Darcy returned low-keyed hellos to him.

John observed them with a laugh. "You look like two cats who swallowed two canaries."

"Something like that," Darcy responded.

Shaking his head, John went into this office and closed the door behind him. Carla dabbed her eyes with a Kleenex, hoping he'd missed their shimmer. Darcy resumed her work at the counter, and Carla stopped playing with pencils and post-it notes and logged onto her computer.

When Marty came out of his office, Carla was close to telling him off for having pushed so many drinks onto her Friday night. With her morning already consisting of Darcy's being too mouthy and Alonzo's being too quiet and John's popping in on her and Darcy's spat, she was on the verge of exploding.

She missed the opportunity for it however as Marty stole the moment by handing her a card, saying, "Sign this, doll. You missed a lunch punch last Wednesday and I've got to get the time cards finished."

Carla signed it and gave it back to him. He winked at her, said thanks, and returned to his office.

Winked? Marty Wilson had never, over all their co-working years together, winked at her. Carla spun her chair around toward Darcy, managing to bang into the wastebasket again, though not knocking it over this time. "You told him, didn't you!"

Darcy shrugged with phony innocence.

Carla left her desk and marched over to her. "You told Marty about—"

"No, I didn't. But maybe, just maybe Alonzo did. Ever think of that? You know how guys talk."

Carla gave a frustrated sigh. Whether Darcy did tell Marty, or Alonzo told Marty, or Marty only seemed to know something but actually didn't…the stress was the same.

"Friday night was a mistake," Carla stated. "A mistake! I don't want Alonzo. I never did. I'm sorry about what happened. He's yours. I think you and he could make a nice couple."

Darcy gave a crude laugh. "Gee thanks. You think I'd want a guy my ex best friend just got done messing with?"

John Milo came out of his office, stopping short upon finding that he'd again walked in on something. He studied his two women employees. "Is there something I should know about?"

At the same time as Carla answered no, Darcy answered yes. John grabbed a schedule sheet off the counter and headed back to his office, shaking his head and muttering to himself. "Mondays…"

Carla returned to her desk and Darcy resumed her work at the counter. They had nothing more to say to one another for now. And it seemed so much better that way.

The first customer of the day came in at nine-thirty. No one acknowledged his approach to the counter. It was like a stand off between Carla and Darcy as to who should wait on him. Both held back rudely. The man cleared his throat, signaling for attention.

It was Carla who gave in first. She swiveled her chair, bumped the wastebasket, got up and approached the counter offering, "I'm sorry. May I help you?"

"Maybe you should learn to help yourself first," Darcy muttered to her.

"Maybe you should just learn to shut up," Carla hissed back at her.

"Should I come back later?" the man asked.

"No, sorry, an office joke thing," Carla apologized.

The shop door opened and Alonzo came out. It shook Carla so much that she dropped her pen. Alonzo picked it up, gave it to her, smiled slightly, then went about his business at the file cabinet.

Darcy was looking at Carla as if she'd dropped her pen on purpose. Carla narrowed her eyes at her as a warning that she'd best not make anything of it.

"Oh, these inside jokes, huh?" the customer commented with a laugh.

Carla turned her attention back to him, feeling more than a little foolish. It was going to be a long day.

Getting out of Milo's at five was the only good thing that came of Carla's workday. It was a grand relief to her, getting home and starting dinner, being in a safer atmosphere. And she was actually hungry. She'd gone into Milo's lunchroom with her bag lunch at noon, but being there and looking around, especially at the sofa in the corner, she'd been unable to eat. She'd ended up tossing her sandwich into the trash container and spending the rest of her lunch time outside strolling around the back parking lot.

Carla was frying hamburgers on the stove when Keith got home. He came up behind her, wrapped his arms around her and gave her a kiss on the back of her neck. She put the spatula down, turned into him and gave him a long kiss on the mouth. He was happily surprised.

"I love you," she told Keith, desperately needing to feel that the two of them were okay.

"Love you, too," he said. Then after another kiss between them, he exclaimed, "And man, am I starving! We started the Hathaway's house today. Worked hard. Your dad insists that we'll have a four-day job done in three days."

Carla handed him a slice of raw onion. "Maybe this will hold you for ten minutes."

He took it, looked at it, grinned, then put it down. "Better not."

He loved onions. His not indulging at this time seemed like a pretty good indication that he was going to make another play for her later. Some kissing in the kitchen was one thing, Carla thought, but she wasn't ready to handle anything more yet.

She felt she no longer had the right to be close to Keith, after having cheated on him the other night. Though could it really be considered cheating? she wondered, trying to shed a different light on it now. It wasn't like her one-night stand with Alonzo had been intentional. She hadn't set out that night to do so. It was a mistake, over and done with like it actually hadn't happened, didn't matter, didn't count. Therefore she really ought to be able to act normal all the way with Keith. It probably wouldn't be easy at first, but she…

Jessie bound into the kitchen. Both Carla and Keith said hi to her, but she said nothing in return. In another of her *new moods* she went to the table, removed her place setting, and put the dishes in the cupboard.

"What are you doing?" Carla asked.

"I'm not eating tonight," the girl stated.

"Too many potato chips after school?" Keith teased.

"Just not hungry," Jessie said.

"You love hamburgers," Carla reminded her.

Jessie left the kitchen, leaving Carla and Keith now exchanging looks of parental concern rather than marital intimacy. There were a lot of surprises, living with a teenager, but amidst them, up until now, Jessie had always maintained a good appetite and a pleasant temperament.

"Probably a boy," Keith rationalized.

Carla shook her head no. "Jessie's like one of them. Romance is a long way off for her yet."

"Shall I go talk to her?"

"No, I will. After you and I finish eating."

"Keith turned up a sly grin. "You mean…like while I'm doing the dishes?"

"Something like that, sure. You offering?"

"Something like that, yeah. But with ulterior motives."

Carla hid her nervousness behind a thin smile, which Keith took as sensual and thus gave a satisfied little growl.

When Carla knocked on Jessie's bedroom door later Jessie called for her to come in, as if she'd been expecting her.

The girl was lying crossways on the bed, watching a video on TV. She shut it off with the remote, and Carla went to sit beside her.

"What's wrong, sweetheart?" Carla asked, affectionately cupping her hand under Jessie's chin.

"I wasn't hungry, okay?" Jessie said defensively.

"You're always hungry. You've got an appetite like your dad's and you—"

"I wasn't tonight."

"Why?" Carla persisted.

"I…I'm on a diet."

"Diet?" Carla gasped.

"I'll grab an apple or something later."

"Jessie, you can't weigh more than a hundred pounds. You certainly don't need to diet. Are you sick? Do you—"

"Okay, I'm not on a diet!" Jessie admitted. "I'm just not hungry. Haven't you ever not been hungry at mealtime?"

"You didn't finish your supper the other night either."

"I'm fine. Honest."

Carla could relate to a loss of appetite more than Jessie could know, which helped her to let up on the girl. She stood up from the bed, hardly satisfied with their little talk but leaving Jessie with, "Go down and get yourself something when you do feel hungry, okay?"

Jessie nodded.

"Love you," Carla turned to tell her before going out the door.

Jessie said nothing.

❧   ❧   ❧

Jessie turned her movie back on the moment her mother left, even though she was no longer interested in watching it now. She merely used it as a cover to mask the call she made on her cell phone.

Three rings were long enough to cause her panic. Ryan had to be home. *Had to.* What if he wasn't? What would she do, where would she turn? If ever she'd needed her big brother, this surely was her neediest of times.

"Ryan!" she blurted his name the second he answered.

"Hey, Jess," he responded with a laugh.

She resented his pleasantness. This wasn't something pleasant. It was the most horrible thing that'd ever happened in her life. "I can't do this," she scowled.

"Do what?"

"Pretend I don't know what Mom did."

"Oh, Jessie…it's a hard one, but you have to."

"It makes me sick to my stomach, seeing her and Dad acting like nothing happened. In the adult world, does that mean cheating can so easily be overlooked?"

"Oh, Jessie…" the big brother said again, this time amidst a sympathetic sigh. "All I know is that you can't make this your business. Neither can I. We have to stay out of it and hope for the best. I know it's difficult for you, living there, but you have to be strong and patient and trusting."

"I don't think I can forgive her for doing this to Dad."

"Does he even know about it yet?"

"I don't think so. I mean, he doesn't act any different than usual. What would it do to him, Ryan, to know? I'm scared, really scared."

"What can I say…do…to make this easier for you, kid?" Ryan gave it some thought and from it eventually suggested, "Get ready. I'll pick you up in a half-hour and take you to a movie? A funny one. Okay?"

She was an avid movie buff and Ryan knew her soft spot well. "I'll be waiting on the front steps," she said.

CHAPTER 7

❀

How convenient, Keith thought, that Jessie should be off to a movie with her brother this evening. He'd so longed to be totally alone with Carla and now they were. Totally. It bothered him that over the weekend she'd often seemed so distant, but tonight was better. Much better. And now, at only nine-thirty, they laid in bed, in each other's arms, talking.

"We weren't supposed to let Jessie do this, you know," Carla said, "go out on a school night."

Keith knew that but excused it. "She's with her brother, that's the exception. They have a special bond, those two. Plus she said she had no homework. And for some reason or other she seemed really down about something tonight. All in all, I think it's okay."

Keith savored the lavender scent of Carla's hair, the softness of her body against his, the deep desire he had for her. Still, after twenty years of marriage, he was passionately in love with and excited over this woman.

He massaged her back and nibbled her neck. Carla's sighs of pleasure were encouraging.

At first, when he started kissing her lips, she was equally eager. But then suddenly she was pushing him away and saying his name like a warning, "Keith…"

He gave her the chance to explain or catch her breath or do whatever it seemed she had to do.

"I'm sorry," was all she said.

"How sorry?" he teased, actually drawing a slight laugh out of her. He slid his hand beneath her nightshirt. When Carla again started to sigh with pleasure, he met her mouth with another kiss.

She didn't stop him this time. Nor did she stop him when he lay atop her and entered her. She rocked and arched and moaned and dug her fingers into his back. It was strange, how after she'd put him off several times recently she now suddenly turned so hot. But it was a strangeness he would not question.

The phone rang in adverse timing. Keith wasn't going to answer it, but Carla urged him to do so.

"Keith, hi, it's Darcy."

"Darcy," he said her name as if a bad taste just came into his mouth.

Carla, lying ultra still on her pillow, looked even more upset than he. No, actually, Keith thought she looked annoyed. *Very* annoyed.

"You there?" Darcy asked of his silence.

"Yeah, I'm here," he told her, passing Carla an *I-told-you-I-shouldn't-have-answered-it* look.

"Gosh, I hope you weren't asleep yet," Darcy said in a sugary voice.

"Oh…no…I wasn't…we weren't." Jeez, for it to be Darcy, of all people, to have made this untimely interruption. For sure Keith wouldn't have picked up the phone if he'd known it was her. He'd never cared for Darcy and only tolerated her as Carla's friend. "So what's up? I suppose you want to talk to Carla."

Not waiting for Darcy to answer, he attempted to hand the phone to Carla. But just that quickly she was out of bed, shaking her head no, and rushing toward the bathroom.

"Well…" he was left to make an excuse for her, "sorry, Darcy. She's uh…indisposed right now. Can I give her a message?"

"Not really," Darcy said, as if maybe her phoning had no actual intention. Though Keith surely suspected it did. "Just tell her I'll see her at work tomorrow."

"Okay." He was ready to hang up.

Except that Darcy continued. "Did she tell you what a good time we had at Milo's party Friday night?"

"I understand Milo's announcement was pretty impressive."

"Oh…yeah…the announcement…right. But as for the rest of the party, we employees had a really good time. Really good."

"Good," Keith said, puzzled at Darcy's tone of necessity.

"Carla didn't tell you that?"

"She said it was nice."

"She didn't give you any details?"

"Details?" Keith resented the game Darcy was obviously playing with him. He never did like her shiftiness, nor did he understand how Carla had always been so blind to it.

Darcy laughed. "Well, anyway, you'll have to get her to tell you more. I'm sure you'd be real interested."

Keith was more annoyed than curious. "It's late, Darcy. If you've nothing more to say then—"

"I've already said it, Keith. The rest is up to you."

Whatever that meant, he thought, frowning as he set the phone back onto the nightstand.

It was a while before Carla came out of the bathroom. And when she did, she had on her robe, which Keith interpreted to mean that their love making was over.

"Anything important?" she asked of Darcy's call.

"I'm suppose to ask you for the details of Milo's party."

Carla's expression went from serious to sickly.

"Why wouldn't you talk to her?" Keith asked.

Carla said nothing.

"It was your idea I answer the phone," he reminded her.

She stood in the middle of the room, tightening her robe belt and looking at the floor rather than him.

"Not to mention," Keith said, "that you and I...we were in the middle of something."

"*Were*," she emphasized.

He studied her, waiting to see what she was waiting for. If she was waiting for him to go drag her back to bed, it wasn't going to happen. The continuation of their intimacy was now up to her. *Damn*, he wished he hadn't answered the phone. And yet, why should it have affected Carla so seriously?

"Want to tell me what this is about?" Keith asked, somehow feeling fearful of finding out.

She obviously didn't, as her reply was, "I'm going downstairs for a glass of milk. Can I bring you some?"

Not waiting for his answer, which would've been a no anyway, she left. What was wrong with this picture? Keith had never known Carla to do this big of a turn around on him. He'd just begun to think that her weekend moodiness was behind them, but evidently not.

He plumped his pillow and slid further down beneath the covers. He closed his eyes, wishing he could close his mind as well. He didn't understand how they'd been making love one minute, then…Surely Carla's emotions were being chastised by something much more than just the weariness of a hectic Monday or Darcy's stupid phone call. But what?

Maybe she was starting menopause, Keith considered. She was almost forty. It would be a little early but not impossible. Yes, that could likely be it. Coming up with a possible explanation soothed his wounded heart enough to make him drowsy. Despite the aloneness of being in bed without Carla, Keith was tired and welcomed the sleep that began to take him.

🍁 🍁 🍁

Carla paced the downstairs in her robe and slippers. A dim living-room light had been left on for Jessie. She would likely be home by ten-thirty. It was now a few minutes past ten. Carla had lied to Keith about wanting a glass of milk. Maybe one of Marty's specials could more likely fill her need, she thought, then hated herself for even thinking it. *God, I've become an alcoholic after one night of drinking.*

She went to the kitchen and opened the refrigerator. She looked inside but found nothing to satisfy her. She opened the back door and went out onto the porch to her swing.

She welcomed the quietness and darkness as an escape from Keith's questions. But she couldn't escape worrying about Darcy's phone call. Though her friend, or rather ex-friend, could not have told Keith anything specific about Friday night, judging from his reaction it seemed she'd planted a good dose of curiosity into him.

It looked like Darcy wasn't going to let up on this. The way she'd stormed over here Saturday morning, the way she'd behaved at work today, her phone call tonight. If only…if only Friday night had never happened. Life had been so sweet and simple for Carla before then. She hated Alonzo for what he'd done to her, yet she couldn't hate herself any less. She hated how Darcy had turned away from her, yet hadn't she surely turned away from *herself*? She felt so lost and alone.

Carla pulled the front of her robe tighter. The night air was chilly, quite a drop from the daytime spring warmth. But there were times, like now, when no other place worked for her like her swing did. It gave her unconditional comfort.

She'd never been so needy of comfort as she was right now. She needed it from Keith, but she didn't deserve it from him. Keith had been the only man she'd ever been intimate with…until now. Until Alonzo. She'd dated Eddie Sherman off and on throughout high school, but there'd been no passion, no sex, no promising future to keep them together after graduation. When Keith happened into her life she'd been a girl with very little experience. Now she'd pushed her experience too far.

Carla wondered what Keith was feeling or thinking or doing upstairs alone in their bedroom. She well imagined he had lots of questions now, ones she wouldn't be able to answer if she went back up there. It was best to stay away. Not easy, but best.

She'd been dozing some when the sound of a car sharpened her senses. A car door closed and footsteps came onto the porch. It was Jessie, home from the movie. Ryan had just let her off in the driveway.

"Mom!" Jessie was startled at first, finding her mother in the swing.

"I wasn't waiting up for you," Carla began as a defense against what she knew Jessie was automatically thinking. "I just couldn't sleep, for no reason, and came down here for a while. It's nice, isn't it? Spring is definitely in the air. How was the movie?"

"Good. Funny. Thanks for letting me go." Jessie stood frozen in place, almost as if she were expecting to get scolded for something.

"Jessie…" Carla began carefully, "you know that you can talk to me about anything at all, don't you?"

Jessie said nothing, as if she weren't sure where this conversation was going but had already decided she didn't like it.

"I mean," Carla added, "we've always been open with one another, and close, you and me."

"Yeah," Jessie halfheartedly agreed.

"Are we? Still?" Carla asked.

"Sure."

Carla got off the swing. "Come on, Jess…what is it?"

"What's what?" Jessie shrugged and looked away from her.

"*That!*" Carla turned the girl's most recent behavior back on her. "That new attitude of yours."

Jessie had nothing to say. Which, to a mother, surely implied there was *something*.

"You're thirteen," Carla said. "I'd like to keep track of what's going on in your life."

"I'm not a baby. I don't need to be tracked. Maybe *you* should be."

"What's *that* mean?" Jessie's remark made Carla awfully uneasy.

And Jessie seemed to well recognize that as she gave a little laugh and said, "Just joking. 'Night, Mom."

It didn't feel like a joke to Carla. Where on earth was Jessie coming from lately? It was a puzzle Carla couldn't solve but couldn't let go.

She stayed on the porch for a while longer, alone with her unending guilt of having missed Jessie's school play. That was what had to be bothering Jessie lately, though the girl refused to admit it. It would be so much easier to get past it if the two of them could just talk about it.

When Carla eventually went upstairs and crawled into bed, Keith asked groggily, "Jessie's home?"

"Yes." She was surprised that he was still awake. "You haven't been to sleep yet?"

"Off and on. I missed you."

Carla wanted to make him feel better but resisted the urge to try.

"You never came back," he said.

"I know," was all she could say.

Keith came closer and put an arm around her. Carla lay absolutely silent and still, a cruel form of rejection. When he rolled back to his side of the bed she felt as much sadness as relief.

Carla was sorry. She knew she was going to be sorry for the rest of her life.

CHAPTER 8

❁

Jessie rang the front doorbell at her grandparents' house Tuesday morning. She was supposed to be at school, but went there instead.

"Jessie! What on earth?" Alice exclaimed when she opened the door. "What are you doing here? What's wrong? Why aren't you at school? Come in, come in."

Jessie entered slowly, meekly, sadly…suddenly wondering if school might've been easier.

Alice took her into her arms and hugged her. "You're trembling, child. What is it?"

"I…I…"

"Oh, Jessie, come sit and tell me."

They sat down together on the couch. Sorry for the scared look she'd brought to her grandma's face, Jessie carefully began, "There's a problem."

"Well, I can see that," Alice sputtered.

It sounded humorous the way she said it, but not enough to lift Jessie's gloom. "This problem…it…I…I can't stand the way it's growing inside me."

"Oh, child!" Alice gasped. "You…you're not pregnant are you?"

"Grandma!" Jessie scowled.

"Well…sorry…the way you said that…and you do have boyfriends…and…but you're too young and—"

"Not boyfriends. Just guys I bike with, that's all. And I'd never do anything so stupid as to get pregnant. Or anything like that. Anyway this…this isn't about me. It's about Mom."

"*Your mom's pregnant?*"

"No. At least, I don't think so. No, I mean…she only…I mean, as far as I know it was only Friday night that she—"

"For heaven's sake, Jessie," Alice's patience snapped, "what is it?"

"My mom…she's having an affair."

"*What*?"

"She had sex with a guy from her work," Jessie said.

Alice shook her head with disbelief. "How do you know this? Or think this? Because it can't be true. Carla isn't that kind of woman. She—"

"She did it, Grandma," Jessie's words picked up speed. "I overheard her and Darcy talking about it in our living room Saturday. It happened Friday night at that company party she was at. *After* the party. Darcy was real mad about it, because this guy was suppose to be *her* guy, and she really told Mom off. And Mom admitted to having done it."

"Oh, Jessie, no," Alice moaned.

"I'm not lying, Grandma."

"You're not a liar, no, I know that. It's just that—"

"Ryan had trouble believing it too."

"Ryan knows?"

"Yes."

"What does he say?"

Jessie shrugged. "He's upset too, but he keeps telling me it's an adult thing and to not dwell on it."

"I could tell you the same," Alice said, "but woman to woman, I know that wouldn't be enough."

At this point Jessie cracked a slight smile. "So what are we going to do, Grandma?"

Alice stood from the couch and took a walk around the room. "I knew Sunday that something wasn't right in your family. I just knew. Your grandpa didn't see it, but I did. What about your dad? Does he know?"

"I don't think so."

"Good, that's good, he shouldn't. Our secret now. Don't you tell him."

"Darcy told Mom that *she* was going to tell Dad if Mom didn't."

Alice sighed and walked some more. "They're friends. She wouldn't do that to your mother. Anyway, let me see what I can do."

As far back as Jessie could remember, her grandma had been like this…ready to step into action when duty called. Especially if the duty was toward a family thing. There was nothing Alice wouldn't do for her family. But this situation would certainly be a challenge for her.

"First," Alice said, pointing a finger at Jessie, "you're not going to get into too much trouble for skipping school, are you?"

"I've got bigger things to worry about right now."

"Yes..." Alice said, studying her, "I guess you do. Okay...so have you had breakfast?"

"A cookie."

Alice frowned. "I'm going to fix you something healthy and—"

"I'm not hungry."

Alice headed toward the kitchen, motioning for her to come along. "I'm going to fix you a bowl of oatmeal, which you will eat whether you're hungry or not, and then I'm going to go have a talk with your mother."

Jessie got off the couch, sighed, and followed her grandmother. It was a customary thing, being fed something to eat whenever you came here. Strangely enough, she felt comforted by that.

🍁 🍁 🍁

"It's Alice," Nathan exclaimed to Keith when he saw his wife's car pull up along the curb and stop before the Hathaway's house they were painting.

"Forget your lunch or something?" Keith asked.

"No," Nathan said on his way down his ladder.

"Forget to kiss her good-bye?" Keith teased.

Somehow Nathan had a more serious gut feeling about this unexpected visit. And when he got to the car and approached Alice on the driver's side, the look on her face intensified his hunch. "This isn't something good, is it?"

She looked at him through the open car window, expressing the answer no without saying a word.

Urging her to speak, Nathan said, "My brush drying."

"Jessie came to our house instead of going to school."

Nathan shrugged. "You want I should phone the principal?"

"She came to tell me that her mom's having an affair."

Nathan's mouth dropped. "Huh?"

"Carla...and a coworker...Friday night."

"You're kidding," Nathan said.

"Would I kid about something like this?"

Nathan took it hard. *No...this couldn't be his Carla. She was so much better than that.* He gazed across the front lawn to where Keith was engrossed with his work. Though his son-in-law didn't appear to have any deep dark problem weighing on him, Nathan nevertheless asked Alice, "Does he know?"

"Jessie thinks not. But she's scared of what if. Keith can't find out, he absolutely mustn't."

"Where's Jessie now?"

"Still at our house. I told her she could spend the day there. She's in no shape to go to school."

"You left her alone? Maybe you—"

"She's all right. She's not two years old anymore, dear. I'm on my way to Milo's to talk to Carla."

"Good idea. I'd like to have a few words with her myself."

"*I'll* talk to her," Alice said, "and that'll be enough."

Nathan looked over at Keith again. "Jeez, how could she do this to him? He's always treated her good, I'm sure. Ain't fair. But I'll talk to him and—"

"No!" Alice said. "I told you he mustn't find out. Don't you say a word to Keith. Nor to Carla. This is a…a woman's thing and I'll handle it. I just wanted you to know, from me, what was going on. But you need to keep it to yourself now, Nathan. Promise."

"You tell me something like this then tell me to keep my mouth shut?"

"Don't make me wish I hadn't told you at all."

Nathan stood frustrated and confused. He looked over at Keith, then back at Alice. Keith again, Alice again. "I don't believe this. *Damn* Carla for her foolishness."

"She's our daughter, Nathan, and we've got to have some compassion for her no matter what."

"And Keith's our son-in-law…what about him?"

Alice dipped her head to look at him through the passenger window. "Let's hope he never finds out."

"No!" Nathan disagreed. "That ain't right. Man's gotta know the truth about what's happening in his family, his marriage, no matter what."

"No!" Alice insisted. "We have to protect him."

"Protect? From the truth? Ain't right. No. I'll talk to Carla and—"

"No you won't," Alice said. "I'll talk to her and you keep quiet."

Nathan stood in a silent stupor.

"Promise?" Alice sought his word.

Nathan couldn't give it.

She started her car. "I'd better go, your brush is drying."

❦   ❦   ❦

Carla sat in her swing savoring some peacefulness and giving herself permission to do nothing more. After Keith left for work and Jessie for school, she'd called in sick to Milo, then came out onto the back porch in her robe with a second mug of coffee. She couldn't face going to work today, not after the way yesterday went. Today she needed time to herself to think and not think as she pleased.

When she heard the front doorbell through the kitchen screen door, it startled her and shocked her into realizing how late it was. Nine-thirty. She left the swing and hurried through the house.

Finding her mother there made her happy and worried both at the same time.

With a scrutinizing look on her face, Alice asked, "May I come in?"

"Of course." Carla opened the door further and stepped aside.

The two of them went into the living room. Alice threw her purse onto the couch, like some sort of temperamental statement, then plunked down beside it. Carla took a chair.

"You're home from work," Alice established.

"Yes. But…but how did you know I was?"

"I went to Milo's to talk to you and they, Darcy, told me you'd called in sick."

"Y-you went to my work?"

Alice sat stiffly, defining her earnestness. "I went there to talk to you, yes, but you weren't there. You were here."

"You went to my work to talk to me?" Carla repeated.

"Are you all right, Carla? I mean, I can understand Jessie's not wanting to go to school, but your not going to work—"

"Jessie?"

"She's at my house. She came there instead of going to school. She's upset, *very upset*, Carla. As you, too, must be. You really are, aren't you."

Alice was studying her so deeply that Carla felt turned inside out. "I'm fine. I want to know what's with Jessie. Mom, what's going on?"

"That's what I came here to ask *you*," Alice said.

Carla shifted in her chair.

"Jessie knows about your affair, that's what's wrong!" Alice blurted out.

Carla went numb for a few moments. Then she stood up, turned in a circle, walked weak-kneed to the front window, looked out, held her head between her hands, felt her mother staring at her back, felt the whole world closing in on her because of Friday night.

"How *could* you?" Alice scolded, as if Carla were fifteen rather than thirty-nine. "I thought your father and I raised you better than this. I thought you were happy with Keith and your children and your home and—"

"Stop it!" Carla said. "It's not about any of that."

"Well, what is it about?"

"It's…how did Jessie know?"

"She overheard you and Darcy talking about it right here in this room Saturday. She'd come home and was in the kitchen."

"So *that's* what's been going on with her." It hit Carla like a ton of bricks. And it made her sick and shameful and crazy with panic. She headed for the kitchen, as in needing an escape. But her mother followed.

"Do you know how devastating it is for a kid to hear that her parent is having an affair?" Alice said, catching up to her.

"One night," Carla clarified. "It was just one night."

"Poor child…what a heavy load she's been carrying. She'd talked to Ryan, but—"

"Ryan knows?" Carla gasped.

"Yes. And about Keith…he…"

"Keith doesn't know! He mustn't know!"

Alice's eyebrows arched. "Well, at least you and I agree on that much."

Carla poured herself some coffee and sank down onto a chair at the table.

"Do you have any idea how sorry I am?"

With amazing tenderness Alice said, "Yes, actually, I think I do. I really, truly do."

Carla realized that her mother was not one of her enemies after all. But somehow that made her feel more sad than happy.

Alice came over to her, bent down and gave her a hug. "I don't like what happened, but however it did I know that it isn't like you and that you must be suffering miserably over it."

Alice started to move away but Carla clutched her hand and kept her close. "What am I going to do, Mom? How can I explain to Jessie? And what about Keith?"

"You've got some explaining to do to Jessie, yes. But you needn't tell Keith."

"Jessie…she's only thirteen."

"Then you speak to her as you *would* to a thirteen year old. Like a mother to her child, about something very serious and not very pretty. You can only be honest with her now. She knows and you can't avoid talking to her about it."

Carla nodded reluctantly. "I know. As for Keith, I'm surprised to hear you say that I shouldn't tell him because that's been my feeling about it too."

Alice smiled, slipped away from Carla's hold and sat down on another chair at the table. "I know you love him, dear. That's what really matters. That's where the truth is. I…I can't see that telling him would be of any benefit to your marriage. Why hurt him over something that can't be changed."

Carla's eyes were tearing. "Right. Exactly the way I see it."

"Good."

"You don't know how good it feels, Mom, to have you on my side."

"Side?" Alice questioned. "I don't think there are any sides here, only good common sense and reasoning. Talk to your daughter and your son, and just go on loving Keith the way you've always loved him. It'll be okay, honey…it'll be okay. Not easy…but okay."

Carla was grateful for her mother's visit. It was a shock, learning that she knew about Friday, but then a relief hearing that she felt the same about not telling Keith. It was more painful for Carla learning that her *children* knew what she'd done that night. But hopefully it would be easier to explain Alonzo to them than to Keith.

Eventually, somewhere down the line in their talk, Alice grinned, tilted her head to one side, and asked Carla, "So this guy…from your work…he's a very appealing man, is he?"

Carla answered out of a weird mixture of embarrassment, shame and pleasure, "Yeah. He is. *Alonzo.*"

"Alonzo," Alice said the name as if that alone played a major part in his appeal.

Carla moaned with a pressing need of telling her mother more. She sipped some coffee and gathered her thoughts ahead of, "I was feeling lousy for having missed Jessie's play. I resented Milo making his event mandatory. I didn't want to be there, but I had to. I…I started drinking a little to…to ease my conscience. And it worked. Sort of. I mean, I never drink. Except for that night."

Alice smiled and nodded, as if she understood all too well.

"And then Alonzo came into the picture," Carla continued her confession, "and I…I guess I was pretty susceptible."

"I guess you were," Alice agreed.

"We danced. He asked me to dance to a really great song playing on the stereo. Keith doesn't dance."

"And that got to you," Alice surmized.

Carla nodded. "We were the only two dancing at the party. The others…they were watching us…and yet it felt like Alonzo and I were the only two people in the room."

"You kind of liked this guy all along, I take it."

"No," Carla answered quickly and firmly. "I mean, not in that way. We worked at the same place but barely paid much attention to each other. Before Friday night."

Carla left the kitchen and went out onto the porch to her swing. Her mother followed and sat with her.

"I'm a terrible person," Carla moaned, "to have lost it like that."

"You're a human being. None of us are perfect."

"You and Dad are. You've been my role models."

"It means a lot to me to hear you say that. Your father and I aren't perfect. But we've tried being good parents, good role models. If we've managed to be that to you then we've succeeded at the most important thing in our lives."

"You've been good ones. I just haven't followed them."

"I love you, Carla," Alice said. "And you're going to get through this just fine. Be kind to Jessie, reassure her that you and Keith are still all right, give her all the solidity you can now. And Ryan…well, he's a big boy."

Carla took a deep breath and let out a long sigh.

"I understand Darcy's threatened to tell Keith if you don't," Alice said.

Carla was amazed. "You know that, too?"

"I wouldn't worry about her. From what I know of Darcy, her talk's pretty cheap." Alice stood up to leave. "Now get yourself together. Get dressed. Take your life back. Act normal, because you *are* normal. This is going to be okay, but only if you make it be. Speak to your kids. Treat Keith the same as always. He doesn't need to know about Alonzo. Forgive yourself. Get on with your life."

Carla swallowed hard, then stood to give her mother a hug. Her mom, bless her, made it sound so simple. Maybe it could be. Maybe.

CHAPTER 9

❈

"So why is Jessie having supper at your parents'?" Keith asked Carla, as just the two of them ate at the kitchen table that night.

"Because..." Carla said hesitantly, "she wanted to, I guess."

Although Keith loved beef stew, he became momentarily more preoccupied with his daughter's absence. "She just had dinner there Sunday, why would she—"

"I don't know." Carla shifted nervously on her chair. Keith was watching, she had to be careful. She gave him a little smile and shrugged.

"Is something wrong?"

"Why would you think that?"

"Jessie's not being here and your being edgy."

"She skipped school today."

"Why?"

"Kids do that now and then."

"Not a good reason."

"How'd your job go today?"

Keith resumed eating. "Hathaway house. Good condition. Light prep work. Your dad was right, we'll finish it tomorrow. Hey, stew's great as usual, honey."

"Thank you." The change of subject helped Carla relax. "I've told you many times, I like the idea of you and my dad working together."

Keith gave her a wry grin. "As in liking me to be where he can keep a close eye on me?"

"Are you saying that you *need* to be watched?" she teased him back.

Ultra serious, Keith pledged, "Baby, I'm yours and only yours, watched or not watched."

Oh, the guilt. Though his saying something like that ought to have made her feel wonderful, it instead made her feel undeserving of his goodness.

Carla pushed her food around on her plate with her fork, hoping Keith wouldn't notice how little of it was actually getting to her mouth. She was glad he was enjoying one of his favorite meals. She loved pleasing him. And she'd always done a good job of it until…

Jessie's empty place at the table was really bothering her more than she let on to Keith. Jessie's knowing about Alonzo, and Keith's not knowing, were equally painful matters in her mind.

The phone rang and Carla nearly jumped out of her skin. Keith went to answer it at the wall unit. Then holding it out to her, he announced, "It's for you. A guy."

Carla left the table and took the phone as if she were being handed a death sentence. "Hello?"

"It's Alonzo," the caller said.

Carla's heart skipped a beat. And then it seemed to rise up into her throat and choke her. Keith sat back down to the table and continued eating while she stood wordlessly holding the phone to her ear.

In a daze she listened to Alonzo explain, "You weren't at work today. John didn't say why. I'm calling to see if you're okay. Are you?"

It wasn't right of him to be calling and checking on her. If it had been anyone's place to do so it would've been Darcy's. Except that Darcy hated her now and wouldn't have lowered herself to phoning. Though Alonzo's intention seemed purely out of thoughtfulness, its happening in front of Keith made Carla feel so exposed.

While Keith was eating, it was obvious how curious he was of Carla's ongoing silence toward her caller. The looks he gave her across the room fed her guilt and made her feel as if he knew all about what happened Friday night and was therefore imagining what this phone call was really about.

"Yes, I'm fine," she finally responded to Alonzo.

"You sure were uneasy at work yesterday."

Though Carla knew Keith couldn't hear Alonzo, she felt as if he could. If only she could say the appropriate thing that would satisfy Keith and Alonzo and herself, all at the same time. The word *good-bye* was on the tip of her tongue.

But Alonzo was already speaking again, "I…uh…just wanted to say that I'm truly sorry."

Carla took a deep breath ahead of telling him, "My husband and I are in the middle of supper."

"Sorry. Won't keep you. It's just that we didn't get a chance to talk yesterday, and your not being there today…well, I got really concerned. I mean…does he know?"

"No, of course not!" Carla said with an unexpected sharpness that made Keith's attention perk all the more.

"Will you be at work tomorrow?" Alonzo asked.

Carla took another deep breath. Then faked a friendly air for Keith's benefit. "Yes, I think so. Thanks for calling. Good-bye."

As she returned to the table, Keith couldn't wait to ask, "Who was that?"

"A…a coworker…from work…"

Though Keith didn't ask for any more of an explanation, Carla knew she owed him one. "I missed work today. He was just calling…for Milo…to see if I was okay and if I'd be in tomorrow."

"You stayed home today?"

"Yes."

"What's wrong?"

"I'm fine *now*. I…I just wasn't so fine this morning, but I'm fine now."

Keith studied her with concern for a few moments then let it go at that. Bless him.

When supper was over he studied her some more, but this time while smiling. "Tell you what…you go sit in your swing, I'll do the dishes, then I'll join you there when I'm done. Okay?"

How could it not be okay? As Carla passed him on her way to the porch, she bent down to kiss the top of his head. "Thanks."

❦   ❦   ❦

Keith didn't mind washing dishes. He frequently offered to do them. Not just when Carla was sick, but many times for no specific reason. What he did mind, mulling it over now as he scoured a pan, was his having found out the way he had about her taking a sick day from work. He'd gotten the distinct impression that she hadn't been intending to tell him, until that phone call, and wasn't comfortable now that she had. And what sense did that make?

They'd been married too long for Keith to not detect when something was wrong. Carla wasn't herself lately. His analysis that she was starting menopause helped him deal with it, but somehow he just didn't feel like he was helping *her* deal with it. Anyway, aware of how much a husband's understanding meant to his wife in that condition, he could at least give that.

He was just finishing the after-supper clean up when Jessie and Nathan came from the front and through the house into the kitchen. Now it was Jessie, who appeared to have a strangeness about her. And there was something noticeably different about Nathan, too. Though Keith felt he sort of had Carla figured out now, it was a whole new puzzle as to what might be up with these two.

"Your hands are red," Nathan observed of Keith.

"I did dishes, the water was hot," he explained to his father-in-law, though his focus was on his daughter. "Jessie, you okay?"

"She's fine," Nathan was quick to say. "She was just hungry for Grandma's beef stew. Weren't you, Jessie?"

"We had stew here tonight also," Keith said.

Jessie gave a *whatever* shrug and turned her look away from him.

"You and I are going to have a talk about your skipping school today," Keith assured her.

Her brown eyes flashed back to him. "Mom told you I skipped?"

"Of course."

"W-what else did she tell you?"

"Just that you were having supper at your grandparents'. Is there more?"

Jessie shook her head no, left the kitchen and headed upstairs.

Keith turned to Nathan. "Is she really okay? Because she doesn't seem too okay to me."

"The kid's fine," Nathan said. "How's Carla?"

Keith gave him an off-sided look. "Why?"

Nathan laughed. "I'm just askin'."

Keith rocked his head. "I'm not sure. She took a sick day from work today, seems a little sluggish, didn't eat much supper. She's out on the porch if you want to see her."

Nathan nodded, started toward the screen door, then stopped and gave a serious look back at Keith. "You two...you and Carla...you're not having a fight, are you?"

Keith blinked his eyes dumbfoundedly. "No. Why would you ask that?"

Nathan reacted a little sheepish, as if maybe he shouldn't have asked. "Aww, I don't know. It's just...you know...things don't always go so smoothly in marriage."

"Carla was sick today and I did the supper dishes. Where do you get a fight out of that?"

"I don't. I'm just askin'."

Nathan went outside onto the porch and Keith stayed in the kitchen, scratching his head in bewilderment.

"I'm going upstairs to talk to Jessie," he called through the screen door. "See ya tomorrow, Nathan, if you're gone before I come back down."

🍁   🍁   🍁

Carla knew exactly what it meant when her father stood there shaking his finger at her and looking so stern. It meant he *knew*. Her mom would've told him, of course. They had no secrets, those two. Carla supposed next her Friday night secret would be broadcast on the TV news and splashed in the newspapers. And then Keith would find out. And then…

"What the hell were you thinking?" Nathan's action turned to words.

Carla began swinging a little faster. She hadn't been scolded by her father since she was a child. And then not often because she'd always been a good kid. She didn't like that he was scolding her now. This wasn't his business. It wasn't anyone's business but her's. Except that because Darcy happened onto it, Jessie'd found out, and then Ryan and then her Mom and then her Dad…not to say that probably everyone at work now knew.

"I'm sorry you found out about it," was the best she could say.

Nathan's anger softened to disappointment. "That's all you can say, that you're sorry I found out? You're not sorry that it happened or—"

"Of course I am! You know me better than that."

"I thought I did."

"I'm still the same person, Dad."

"No you're not. You're not the same by any means. You cheated on your husband. Keith's a good guy. You had no right to do that to him."

"I didn't do it *to* him."

"That's right," Nathan sneered, "you did it to some other guy."

Oh, this talk was so uncomfortable, so degrading, so unreal. Carla felt so very dirty in the eyes of her father.

"I mean, I didn't set out to hurt Keith. And…and he won't get hurt because he's not going to find out about this."

Nathan was shaking his finger at her again. "Oh, yes he is. He has a right to know."

"No."

"I'm looking at this from a man's point of view, Carla, a husband's. Keith has to know."

"What good would it do?"

"It would keep honesty in your marriage for one thing."

"Not telling him isn't the same as lying to him."

"Some secrets are the same as lies, Carla. I think a lot of Keith, you know, and I won't stand by and let him be in the dark about this."

Carla rose out of the swing, insisting, "He's not going to know."

Nathan studied her but kept his resolve. "We'll see about that. We'll just see about that."

"You're turning on me?" she asked, feeling far worse now than when Darcy had turned on her.

"You're the one who took the turn, girl. One hell of a wrong one. And you're the only one who can attempt to right it."

"You think something like this can be righted?"

"You know what I mean." Before Nathan walked off the porch, he gave her one more piercing look. "Be honest with him, Carly. You owe him that."

It was not long after Nathan had left that Keith came downstairs and out onto the porch. He too looked laden with disappointment. Carla supposed his talk with Jessie had been trying. He sat down beside her in the swing.

"She promised not to skip again," he concluded of their daughter.

"Good," Carla said.

"She told me the reason why she did."

"Really?" Carla's voice quivered.

"She said she wasn't prepared for her English test and couldn't face it."

Carla was relieved at Jessie's lie, only because the truth would have been so much worse. She shivered at the irony.

Keith put an arm around her. "Cold?"

"Not anymore," she said, snuggled against him. "Thanks for doing dishes."

"You're welcome. There'll be a slight service charge."

"I should've known. How much?"

"Ah-ha..." he said, giving her a self-explanatory squeeze. "Did you notice that your dad seemed a little testy tonight?"

"No," Carla lied.

"Well, maybe it was just me." Keith kissed her. "So how *you* doing?"

"I'm okay. Better than this morning. Just tired."

"Yeah, me too." Keith pretended to yawn. "Think I'll go upstairs, get a shower, and do some reading in bed."

"I'll be up in a while," she told him.

He kissed her more deeply this time, then left.

A few minutes later Jessie came out onto the porch to join Carla. She kept her distance, leaning against the railing, quietly staring into space for a time. She wasn't going to bring up the subject of Friday night, even though the pain of it was clearly imprinted on her sad face.

It was going to be Carla's job to start it rolling, as much as she dreaded to. "Grandma told me about your going to her place this morning instead of school."

Jessie said nothing. She wasn't going to make this easy for Carla.

Carla stopped the motion of the swing and leaned over her knees toward Jessie. "She told me the reason for your going there. The real reason. It wasn't about an English test you couldn't face."

"How *could* you?" the girl found her voice.

"You're thirteen, you're way too young to even begin to understand, but I—"

"I understand that you cheated on Dad. I understand that and it stinks."

"Jessie, I told you I had to miss your school play Friday because the Milo event was extremely important and—"

"Yeah...like having sex with some guy you work with."

Feeling as if she'd just been slapped in the face, Carla got off the swing and went to her daughter, pleading, "Listen to me, please, Jessie. I had to go to the dinner meeting. Had to. It was important."

"And where did the sex fit in?"

"There was drinking at the party. Oh, Jessie...I'm not a drinker but I started having a few and...oh, Jessie, please tell me that you won't ever touch the stuff. It does awful things to you."

"We're talking about you now, aren't we? Not me."

"Things change when you drink excessively. I...I wasn't myself. This guy and I...we didn't mean to...I mean...oh, Jessie, this is so hard to explain."

The girl shrugged coldly and her voice hardened. "What is, is. What's to explain?"

"There are no excuses, but there are reasons. I am so sorry. Believe me. I need your understanding and love and—" Carla started to put her hand on Jessie's arm, but Jessie flinched away.

"Dad doesn't deserve this," the girl stated.

"No, he doesn't," Carla could only agree. "I love him. What I did had nothing to do with him."

"Maybe you're right," Jessie conceded, "about my being too young to understand. Because I don't think I understand the word love at all."

She went inside the house, and Carla went back to the swing, bursting into tears.

🍁　　　🍁　　　🍁

Propped against his pillows in bed, Keith was only a few pages into chapter two of his new sci-fi novel when Carla came upstairs. Good. He'd been more absorbed in waiting for her than in what he was reading.

Now that she was here, however, he felt more saddened than happy for the down-hearted spirit she brought with her. He realized what an ordeal menopause was. He wanted to comfort her and tell her that he'd be there for her all the way. But he somehow felt it might be better to let her tell him about her condition in her own time.

Maybe this was going to be that time, he thought, as she came to sit beside him on the edge of the bed. He closed his book and put it aside. The two of them exchanged solemn looks. Words seemed hard to come by for both of them.

Finally Keith decided it was, after all, up to him. "I want you to know," he began gently, "that I know."

If he thought Carla had looked sickly before, it was nothing compared to now. Her face turned pale, eyes dismal, and voice quivery. "Y-you know?"

"Yeah, I figured it out. And I want you to know that I'm going to be patient and understanding and will love you just the same no matter what."

"What are you saying?" Carla still needed to ask.

Keith put his arms around her and held her. "I'm trying to tell you that you've got nothing to worry about, honey."

"Worry about?" she questioned.

She was probably embarrassed that he came to such a conclusion on his own before she herself got around to telling him. Anyway he'd started it thus he'd best go all the way with it. "Menopause."

"*What*?" She drew back from him.

He realized then that he shouldn't have brought up the touchy matter to her. "It's okay, honey. It doesn't mean to me that you're getting old. It just—"

On her rush to the bathroom, Carla stated, "I'm not in menopause! How could you think that? I'm not even *forty* yet!"

Keith puffed his cheeks then released a hard puff of air. He'd been wrong in diagnosing her. *Boy, had he been wrong.* He'd only meant to be observant and understanding, but instead he'd put himself in deep shit. Okay, well, so what then could it be that was affecting Carla lately? If not menopause, he had no other idea. He only knew that when things weren't right with her they weren't right with him.

It felt almost like she was hiding something from him. Something that was eating away at her that she couldn't tell him about. Maybe she'd bought another expensive dress, like that beige one that she'd paid a fortune for some time ago. Or maybe she'd dented her car. He'd take a look at it in the morning. Forget menopause. He would have to start viewing this from a whole different perspective.

CHAPTER 10

❊

It was Wednesday and Carla had to go to work. She'd stayed home yesterday but couldn't do that again today. Things were the way things were and she had to deal with the reality she'd created.

A half-hour ago Jessie went off to school in a huff that Keith didn't understand. And then before he left for his job Carla kissed him with a fervor he also didn't understand, following last night. Poor Keith, though he could probably relate Jessie's recent behavioral changes to her simply being a teenager, his assessment of Carla's recent mood swings had been dead wrong.

She wasn't starting menopause. How could he think that? She was way too young. Except for a little anxiety lately she wasn't having hot flashes or night sweats or weight gain. At least she didn't think…

Turning this way and that, she studied herself in the bedroom mirror. She clasped her waist, then smoothed her hands down over her hips. She patted her stomach, verifying that her paisley knit skirt fit as well as it always had. Next Carla leaned across the dresser for an extreme close-up in the mirror. She ran a fingertip just above her upper lip and squinted carefully at the area with satisfaction.

She wasn't into menopause. No way, not yet. Thank goodness she didn't have that to deal with along with her *infidelity*. It was obvious that Keith felt something unusual was going on with her lately, but he would never know the truth of it. The kids knew, unfortunately. She'd now had a talk with Jessie about it, which hadn't gone well. It was painful seeing such indignation in her daughter's eyes. Carla supposed when she talked to Ryan about this he would look upon her in the same way. But Keith, he must not find out about Alonzo. Not ever.

Darcy, busy at the counter when Carla arrived at Milo, glanced up briefly and spoke a cool, "Good morning."

Carla gave a nod and said nothing. Despite the strain between them she couldn't help noticing, as she did quite routinely, how beautiful Darcy was. She envied her ultra thick, dark hair, expressive dark eyes, voluptuous figure, and flare for fashion. Today Darcy was wearing long dangle earrings, tight aqua slacks, and a black, sequined, scoop-neck sweater exposing some cleavage. *Carla* had some cleavage…hidden behind her crisp, white, buttoned-up blouse.

"Feeling better today?" Darcy asked in a manner of not actually caring.

Carla sat down to her desk and put her purse in the side drawer.

Her silence was enough for Darcy to add, "Yeah, well, you'd better snap out of it because there's lots to do. We fell behind yesterday, with you being out."

"Sorry," Carla apologized.

"How innocently you say that."

"I'm *very* sorry," Carla added.

"Which really doesn't change a damn thing, does it?"

"I can't go backward, if that's what you mean." Carla logged on to her computer and checked her inbox.

"You make me sick," Darcy scowled.

"Well, you made me sick enough yesterday that I couldn't even come to work," Carla dished it back at her.

"Might it have been Alonzo, not me, that's bothering you?"

"Stop it! Shut up, Darcy, just shut up!" Carla was in the midst of shouting when the side door opened and Alonzo came out of the print shop into the front office.

Realizing he'd intruded on something personal between the two women, he lowered his eyes and walked over to the counter without speaking. He took an order slip out of the workbasket then quickly went back to the shop.

As the door closed behind him, Carla breathed easier.

But Darcy couldn't wait to exclaim, "My goodness, he hardly acts like the man who'd made passionate love to you just a few nights ago."

"Stop it!" Carla said through gritted teeth.

"Must be terribly disappointing for you."

"Is this the way it's going to be now?" Carla asked. "Your attacking me every chance you get? If you're this bold why don't you just go after Alonzo and throw yourself at him? Maybe he'd like that. Men seem to like that, Darcy, and if my memory's correct you've thrown yourself at quite a few since your divorce. Please don't let me get in the way of you and Alonzo. He's yours for the taking."

"Gee thanks, as if I'd ever want him now." Whatever Darcy was searching for in a counter drawer she couldn't find and thus blurted out a string of cuss words in frustration.

"It was a mistake, a stupid mistake," Carla insisted. "Nobody's more sorry than I am over it."

Darcy straightened up, took a deep breath and sneered back at her. "Not even Keith? Because…he does know about it by now, doesn't he?"

Carla said nothing.

"Well, that's another stupid mistake of yours," Darcy said, assuming her answer. "So I guess telling Keith will have to be my job."

"I'll take care of my husband in my own way."

Darcy was shaking her head. "You cheated on him and you have a consequence to pay."

"Stay out of this," Carla warned.

The shop door opened and Alonzo returned. He exchanged his paper for another out of the basket. "Grabbed the wrong one before. Guess catching you girls in the middle of a fight threw me off a little."

Carla silently counted to ten then started applying herself earnestly to her work. She used to love coming to work. Now, since Friday, it was horrible. Maybe she could get over Friday night's happening if Darcy would just let up on her about it. If she could just get through this day at work. And then tomorrow. And the rest of her life. One day at a time. One hour. One minute. She glanced at the wall clock above her desk. It was but nine-fifteen.

Carla became unglued all over again when Marty came out of the back office into the front. The look he gave her made her feel like a prostitute. Surely it meant he knew about her and Alonzo.

On his way to the water cooler he chirped, "'Morning, girls. My, my the two of you look stunning this morning."

His cheerfulness was phony, way overplayed. If he was purposely trying to antagonize Carla, it worked.

"What were you putting into those drinks you made for me Friday night?" she asked in the tone of demand.

He chuckled. "Sugar and spice and everything nice."

Carla got out of her chair. "You knew I wasn't a drinker, yet you kept making me stuff that went down all too easily."

Marty drank his water then dropped the empty paper cup into the wastebasket. "I'm a damn good bartender, that's all. I please my customers. You were definitely pleased that night, far as I could tell."

"She's trying to blame you for where those drinks led her," Darcy told Marty. "It's about what went on after—"

"That's enough!" Carla warned her.

"Ah-ha…" Marty said, all too knowingly.

Carla sank back down to her desk, tempted to crawl under it. Marty laughed and went back to his office.

Darcy took the stack of morning mail off the counter, brought it over to Carla and dropped it on her desk. "Here, these need to be stamped and sorted."

"You told him, didn't you," Carla said through gritted teeth.

"Maybe I did and maybe I didn't," Darcy replied smugly.

Carla picked up the envelopes, held them, stared at them, and was in no mood to deal with them. She slammed them back down on her desk, telling Darcy, "Screw the mail! Screw you! I thought you were my friend. How could you do this to me? How?"

Darcy's laugh was haunting. "Me? Do to you? You hung yourself, sister."

Carla got up, took her purse out of the drawer, grabbed her jacket off the back of her chair and marched around the counter toward the front door. "I'm outta here!"

She stormed outside and ran around the building to her car in the back parking lot. Anguish pounded in her head. Surely she was going crazy. Her whole world was crumbling and she couldn't stop it. And being sorry didn't seem to matter. And she couldn't work at Milo Printing anymore, she just couldn't.

🍁   🍁   🍁

"What's with you today?" Nathan asked his son-in-law as they worked together that morning.

Keith was on a high wrung of his ladder, painting under the eaves of the house, while Nathan worked below on the window trim. Keith gazed down to meet Nathan's curious look. "Nothing."

"You've hardly spoken a word since we started."

"I'm a quiet person, you know that."

"Something's bugging you."

"Yeah," Keith laughed, "*you*."

Holding his paintbrush idle, Nathan narrowed his eyes seriously at Keith. "She told you, didn't she?"

"Who? What?" Keith had no idea where his father-in-law was coming from.

Nathan turned silent and resumed his painting, almost as if maybe he'd accidentally said too much about something he shouldn't have. But he wasn't going to get out of it that easily. Whatever he'd almost opened up with, Keith needed to make him finish.

Keith backed down from the ladder and planted his feet on the ground close to Nathan. "Who? What?"

"Nothin'," Nathan muttered.

"Don't tell me nothin'!"

"And don't tell me I can't *say* nothin'."

"You started something, now finish it."

"It's finished."

"Like hell." Keith knew that for Nathan, an avid talker, to hold back on something this way, it had to be serious. And difficult. And probably something bad.

As Keith waited him out, his mind wandered back to earlier that morning at home and the strangeness of his wife and daughter. What had happened to Jessie's cute, bubbly spirit? And what was going on behind Carla's hot and cold moods if it wasn't menopause? And now...he studied his father-in-law, wondering why he, too, was behaving so strangely.

Nathan laid his brush across the top of his paint can, walked over to the Hathaway's front porch, and sat down on a step.

Keith followed him. "Taking a break already?"

"Taking a break," Nathan verified. Then sadly he added, "Aww, Keith, damn it...you don't deserve this."

Keith's patience snapped. "Are you going to tell me what you already thought I knew but I don't...or am I going to have to kick your butt a few times to get it out of you?"

Nathan laughed. "Can't kick my butt when I'm sitting on it."

"I can pull you off those steps and pretend you're not my beloved father-in-law."

Nathan grinned. "Beloved? *Whoa.*"

The chubby little Mrs. Hathaway came out the front door carrying a plate of cookies. "Saw you boys taking a break and thought you might like these."

"Oh, yes, thanks." Nathan helped himself to one.

Keith didn't want a cookie but took one out of politeness.

"What a beautiful day for painting," the woman said, as if it were a gift to behold.

Nathan assured her, "We're only taking a little break here. We're not goofing off. Your house will be done and pretty as a picture by five o'clock."

She giggled and shooed a hand at him. "Goodness...I'm not keeping time on you boys. Take as many breaks as you like. Finish off these cookies. I've another batch in the oven."

When the woman went back inside the house, Keith started in on Nathan again. "I want to know who *she* is and what she *told* me, which whoever she is she didn't."

Nathan gave him a dumbfounded look. "Huh?"

Yes, it *was* a beautiful day, Keith realized, trying to admire it in the way Mrs. Hathaway had. The trees were budding, the air was fresh, the sun was radiating its wondrous energy. He shouldn't be driven by things he didn't understand. He needed to let them go and get the best out of his day.

Nathan was still giving him that stupid, mysterious look, but Keith wasn't going to let it bother him anymore. He grabbed another cookie and started across the lawn to his ladder.

"That's it?" Nathan called after him, almost as if he'd hoped for a longer confrontation.

A dedicated worker with plenty of work awaiting him, Keith gave up. He didn't have to waste time trying to make something out of the mind games his family seemed to be playing on him lately. He could ignore them and choose to think positive.

On his way to the ladder, Keith caught sight of Mrs. Hathaway looking out a window. He waved at her, and she smiled and waved back at him.

"Stop flirting and start painting," Nathan jokingly ordered, coming along behind him.

"She makes very good cookies," Keith said.

🍁 🍁 🍁

"You can't do this, Jessie," Ryan told her as she plowed into his apartment toting a duffel bag.

She'd dawdled around some at the arcade after school before coming there, hoping by then Ryan would be home from work. How good she'd felt on her approach, seeing his car in the lot. Now if only he himself were a little more welcoming.

"Would you rather have me out on the street?" she asked.

"I'd rather have you back home with Mom and Dad where you belong."

"You're my brother, you can't turn me down."

"I can if I want to."

Jessie went to the kitchen and helped herself to an apple off the counter. She took one bite, made a face, and put the remainder back in the bowl.

"Don't do that," Ryan said. "You started that apple, now finish it. They cost money, you know."

"I'm not hungry, just nervous. I'm going crazy and you don't even care."

The brother sighed and shook his head. "I know this is hard, but—"

"I'm staying!" Jessie kicked off her shoes, walked past him and curled herself up on the couch.

Ryan studied her sadness until he began to believe it. "Okay…you can stay for supper, that's it."

"Our family is wrecked, don't you realize that?"

"Look, I don't like what happened either," Ryan said, "but life goes on. When you become an adult, you accept that."

"Life sucks."

"Sometimes, yeah." Ryan sat down next to her and gave her an affectionate hug.

Maybe, Jessie thought, if he were a girl, or at least not yet an adult, he'd be as upset as she was. Anyway, for whatever way he was taking this, she was more glad than she'd ever been over having a big brother with his own place.

They talked for a while about stuff that led them nowhere. Yet in a way it seemed to help them both. At least it was all they could do for now.

Ryan was startled when a knock came at his door. He almost looked scared of answering it. When he did get up to do so, he took his time getting there.

Though Jessie couldn't see who it was from where she sat, the visitor he met in the doorway had a woman's voice. Ryan didn't invite her in, they just stood there talking in low, secretive voices. Jessie strained to hear what was being said, but nothing was clear enough for her to understand.

Curiosity soon drove her to leave the couch and sneak over to a place of better viewing and listening. A glimpse showed her that Ryan's visitor definitely was a woman, not a girl. With her hair done up in a bun, and wearing a black skirt and jacket suit, she looked business like, sophisticated, out of his league.

"Yeah, my sister," Ryan whispered, as if he were assuring the woman for a second time.

She whispered something back to him, of which Jessie managed to make out only the word *later*. Then Ryan pulled the woman into his arms, gave her a kiss, and also said the word *later*.

When his fly-by visitor left, Ryan shut the door and turned around, both surprised and annoyed at finding that Jessie'd been eavesdropping.

He offered no explanation. And for as curious as Jessie was, she didn't ask. She had enough to worry about right now, without adding Ryan's love life. She returned to the couch and curled up in silence.

Heading for the kitchen, Ryan said, "I feel like a hot chocolate. How about you?"

"Make mine a double," she replied.

CHAPTER 11

❀

"He knows," Nathan said to Alice as they sat in the living room after dinner.

Alice looked up from her needlework and grinned. She was crocheting a baby blanket for the young couple next door that was expecting their first child in June. "Knows? Who? What?"

"Keith knows about Carla's infidelity but is pretending he doesn't."

Alice transferred her bundle of yarn from her lap to the footstool and studied Nathan solemnly. "No, he can't possibly know."

"Today…the way he looked…acted…"

"Which tells you he knows?"

"You had to be there," Nathan said. "But yeah, I'm sure that's what's going on with him. He was a different person today. Like something really had a hold on him. Like what else could it be?"

Alice shook her head. "Well, it can't be that because Carla vowed she was never going to tell him."

Nathan sprung out of his chair as though he'd been jabbed from behind. "What do you mean she's never going to tell him?"

Alice left her chair more gracefully, and the two of them stood before one another in confrontation. "Carla decided not to tell Keith, therefore I'm sure he doesn't know."

Nathan grasped his head and moaned. "Stupid!"

"It's not."

"It is. Alice, that is so wrong."

"To protect Keith?"

"To keep the truth from him. If, in fact, she has. I mean, maybe she—"

"This isn't even our battle, is it," Alice tried to end the conversation there.

"Which is why you couldn't wait to rush over and have a mother-daughter talk with Carla as soon as you heard about her indiscretion, right?"

"Don't you care about those two? Don't you want what's best for them?"

"Truth is always the best," Nathan stood his ground. "Okay, if not for Keith how about for Carla. Our daughter cheated on her husband. She doesn't need to be a liar besides."

Alice sat down and started crocheting again.

Nathan stood near, watching her, waiting for her to see his side of reasoning. "That's going to be a nice blanket."

"Thank you."

"Carla's not behaving like the daughter we raised."

"Our daughter loves her husband."

"Enough to tell him the truth?" Nathan contended. "She messed up. She has to pay the consequence."

"Telling Keith is not her consequence."

"Okay, well then maybe *I'm* her consequence. You obviously had a persuasive, motherly talk with her, now I need to have a persuasive, fatherly talk with her."

Nathan left the living room, heading for the den.

Alice followed, shrieking, "No! You're not calling Keith!"

"That's right," he said, lifting the desk phone, "I'm calling Carla. I'm going to tell her to tell Keith the truth or I will."

Alice grabbed the phone away from him and slammed it back onto the receiver. "You can't do that. What Keith doesn't know won't hurt him. Not as much as his knowing would."

Nathan didn't understand Alice's desperation. Only his own. He reached for the phone again.

"Leave them alone!" she shouted so loud it made him blink.

Nathan took a deep breath. "You and I haven't had an argument in years. I'm not liking this, Alice."

"Then back off of this matter," she advised him. "I've got a headache. I'm going upstairs to lie down."

Nathan wasn't about to drop it that easily. He followed her, talking all the way. "It's not a headache. It's stubbornness. Open your eyes, woman. Carla's keeping this from Keith is a worse sin than what she did to him in the first place."

Rather than going to the bed, Alice sat down on the bedroom window seat. Nathan went to stand beside her. Together they looked out at the big oak tree that seemed to own the front yard. And the flagstone walkway they'd just put in last year that meandered its way beneath it from the street.

"I love this house and yard," Alice said.

"Me too," Nathan said.

They were quiet for a few minutes, until Alice reopened their disagreement. "Why can't you just leave this up to Carla to handle?"

"Why couldn't you?" he asked her back. "You went running right over to give her advice that was totally out of line. So what do you call that?"

Alice sighed. "I'm tired."

"Me too." Nathan kissed the top of her head then headed for the phone on the nightstand. "Why don't you get ready for bed. I'll make a quick call to Carla then we'll turn in."

Alice came after him in a rage. "You are *not* going to phone her!"

"Did you mean that to sound like an order?" he verified, barely recognizing his wife as the wife he knew. Carla's situation was already contorting their lives, if not Keith's yet.

"Yes," she said.

"Well, I ain't taking it," Nathan said. "I work with Keith every day, and maybe I'm feeling more concerned over him in this mess than I am over Carla."

"Exactly why you have to protect him!" Alice argued.

"Exactly what I'm trying to do," he said.

Alice screamed, as if she were in dire pain, "No! No! No!"

Nathan was starting to wonder now if besides the Carla/Keith problem he might have something totally separate in his very own marriage to be concerned about.

"I need you to listen to me," she said, quieting down to a wearisome whisper.

He gave her a silent go-ahead nod.

Alice sat down on the edge of the bed and he sat beside her.

"It's time," she said, giving him a look even stranger than any of those she'd already given him that evening. "And...you're not going to like this."

"Yeah, I'm getting that," Nathan responded.

"The reason I don't want you being so hard on Carla over this is because—"

"She cheated on her husband," Nathan rallied again, "and you're defending that."

"I'm not defending it. It's just that...I...I do know she didn't mean to do what she did and—"

"Come on, Alice, you're not going to say it was an accident. That sort of thing doesn't just simply *happen* like the romance novels infer. Carla's a big girl, a smart girl, a good girl. If she—"

"Things happen to those sort of girls too," Alice fended.

"Why do I get the feeling you're trying to say something beyond what we're really talking about?"

"Because I am," she admitted. "Because this isn't easy." She laid her hand on Nathan's knee, looking close to crying, scaring him more and more by the minute. "I never wanted to tell you this, Nathan, but…the same thing happened to me as it did to Carla."

He drew a blank. Like if he was supposed to be adding his own thinking into what she'd just said, he couldn't, he was too stunned.

Alice spelled it out for him, "I never intended to cheat on you."

Nathan opened his mouth, but no words came.

"It just happened," she continued. "And I felt really bad. And I didn't want to hurt you. I wanted to spare you the hurt, because I knew it was something I would never do again. I honestly thought it was best to never tell you. And it proved to be the best. Until now. And…and this problem now surfacing between you and me only proves the old saying, *what you don't know won't hurt you.* Right? Now that you know? And…and that's why I don't want Keith to find out about Carla. It doesn't help matters, it only makes it worse. Right? Can't you can see that now?"

Nathan's eyes narrowed, and it took all the effort he had to ask, "You cheated on me? When? Who? Why?"

She gave a nod. "Forty one years ago."

Nathan stood up, feeling sick to his stomach.

"This is what you want Keith to go through?" Alice verified.

"You *cheated* on me?" Nathan was still stuck on that much.

She stood up face-to-face with him. "And weren't you better off for not knowing it all this time? Up until now?"

"Who was it Alice? Who was the guy that lured you away from your new husband? Because, as I count, forty-one years ago we were pretty newly married."

"A name doesn't matter."

"*It does.*"

"Wayne."

It was a bad dream, growing worse, that Nathan wasn't waking up from. "My best friend, Wayne? Jeez, Alice!"

"We'd had a fight, you and me," she started to explain, as if there could actually be a reason. "I was young and hurt and needed comfort."

"I was your husband. You were supposed to turn to *me* for comfort."

"I know. It was a mistake. A terrible mistake. Don't you think I know that, haven't lived with self-punishment over it all these years? I kept the pain to myself to spare you."

"Again...I was your husband, Alice, we were suppose to share everything...good, bad, and indifferent."

She sat back down on the bed with a sigh. "There...there's still more to it."

"Like it went on for years and years behind my back?"

"No," she said, with tears in her eyes and a choke in her voice. "It...it was only once."

"*Only*," he stressed the word.

"I...I want you to know that I'm only bringing this up now for Carla and Keith's sake. You need to know the damage some truths can do."

"Truth is never the enemy, Alice."

She was having trouble looking him straight in the eye but forcing herself to do it along with saying, "Carla...she...Wayne's the biological father."

It took Nathan a long time to absorb what he'd just heard. His mind seemed to spiral around and down into some deep, dark place of denial. The word *no* helped to soothe him. No, no, no.

Alice waited quietly, watching him.

Finally Nathan verified out loud, "I'm...not Carla's father?"

"Oh, yes, Nathan, you are, in the very best respect," Alice spoke ever so gently, as if that might help. "I didn't want to hurt you, not then, not now. But we're old, and Carla and Keith have a lot of years ahead of them. They don't need the pain of—"

"A lie is a lie," he said, "whether it's up front or hidden for years. "You should've told me up front, Alice. It...it only gets worse over time, can't you see that?"

"I'm trying to prove a point here."

He nodded. "That you have. Except now tell me, how can you assume Carla is Wayne's after having supposedly been with him only one time?"

"Carla's blood type. It showed that you weren't the father. If you weren't the father then it had to be him. I couldn't believe it. It was so unfair, my being with him only once and my being with you all those—"

"Unfair...yeah...something like that," Nathan muttered out of his fogginess. "We lived a lie...all those years."

"I suffered the lie, you didn't."

"And how much did Wayne suffer?"

"I never told him about Carla being—"

"Strange, how one day he just up and moves his life to Italy. I guess...maybe...now it makes sense."

"He didn't know about the baby," Alice said. "His move was because of his job. You *know* it was."

Nathan gave her a slanted look. "Do I? And because his job takes him to another country he drops all contact with his old friend Nathan?"

Alice said nothing. And Nathan almost felt some peace in the nothingness. He went to the closet, pulled out a duffel bag and started throwing some of his things into it.

"What are you doing?" she asked excitedly.

"What's it look like?"

"You're not leaving! Not when you forced me to—"

"I may have forced you to speak a long overdo truth, Alice, but I certainly didn't force you to shack up with Wayne."

Nathan left the bedroom, trying not to care that he left Alice standing there looking so desolate. But she could not be any more desolate than he was right now. He tried not to care that this was the end of a forty-one year marriage and all the trust he'd put into it.

It felt good, jumping into his truck. Even better backing out of the driveway. At last he could let his own tears fall.

❦   ❦   ❦

Carla woke up somewhere in the middle of the night and couldn't get back to sleep. After just so much tossing and turning she gave up, slipped out of bed, and went downstairs.

It was ultra quiet and dark on the back porch. She sat in the swing, taking its comfort, acquiring a calmness she'd lacked in bed. She breathed deeply of the cool night air. Looking out beyond the porch roof at the stars in the sky helped make her problems seem less significant and herself more humble.

Later, as Carla grew drowsy and almost ready to try going back to bed, the kitchen light went on and cast a yellow path out through the screen door and across that end of the porch. She heard the refrigerator door open and a clinking of dishes.

Soon Jessie came wandering out onto the porch carrying a bowl of ice cream and a spoon. She wasn't startled, seeing her mother there in the swing. Since the kitchen's heavy inner door had been open, Carla's being in the swing had been inevitable to her.

Nevertheless she asked, "What are you doing?"

"Swinging. Couldn't sleep. What are you doing?"

"Ice cream. Couldn't sleep. Want some?"

"Sure."

Jessie went back inside then soon returned with a bowl of ice cream and a spoon for her mother.

"Thanks." Carla took a spoonful into her mouth. "Mmm…chocolate chip, my favorite."

"I know. Mine too."

Jessie, in her pajamas and fuzzy slippers, sat on the railing. Carla, in the swing, had a sweater on over her nightgown. Eating ice cream together seemed to put them on common ground. At least for a while.

"Aren't we silly?" Carla tried making light of quiet that came between them. "Sitting here shivering and eating ice cream."

Jessie's pleasantness was gone. "There's nothing silly about my being unable to sleep and your being unable to sleep. I hate what's happening in this family."

"Jessie…" Carla began, slowly and tenderly, "all families have problems to deal with at some time or another."

"How many families have mothers who are having affairs?" Jessie lashed out at her.

"I'd give anything if you hadn't found out about that," Carla said, on the verge of losing her own composure. "It…Jessie, it wasn't what you think."

"I don't have to think. I heard Darcy perfectly well that day."

"Darcy exaggerates."

"How can you exaggerate sleeping with someone? Either you did or you didn't."

"Well…yes…but…"

"Are you and Dad going to get divorced?"

Carla got out of the swing and walked over to Jessie. "What Dad and I do is nothing you need to worry about."

"Yeah right…like whatever you guys do doesn't effect me."

The mother and daughter shared close looks but distant thoughts. Despite the lack of light, Carla saw a shimmer in her daughter's eyes. Just a short while ago there'd been tears in her own eyes. How could she make Jessie feel better when she felt so awful herself? Right now, this moment, soothing the matter felt like an impossible feat.

"I'm going back to bed," Jessie said, leaving the railing and hurrying inside.

Alone again in the silence of the middle of the night, it was no longer a peaceful retreat for Carla. Not after her confrontation with Jessie. She was more jittery now than when she'd been sleepless in bed earlier.

Carla longed for someone to be on her side. But there was no one she could talk to, really talk to, about her mistake. More than anybody she needed Keith, but unfortunately he was the last person she could talk to about this. She needed a friend, but Darcy was a definite out. She needed her *mother*. A woman was never too old to need her mother.

Carla went inside and phoned her parents' house.

"Nathan?" Alice answered.

"Mom, it's Carla."

"Oh…uh…Carla. *It's two a.m.* What's wrong?"

"Maybe I should be asking you that. Why did you think it was Dad calling? Mom, what's going on over there?"

"He left."

"What do you mean he left?" Though Carla had made the phone call in hopes of feeling better, it was going the opposite way. "Mom?"

"We…had a little fight, your dad and me. He walked out a few hours ago. I haven't been to bed."

"You and Dad never fight. What happened?"

The line went silent for a few moments. Then Alice said softly, "Carly…never mind us. Are *you* okay?"

"I don't know. No, especially not after having called you."

"It's the middle of the night," Alice established. "You wouldn't be calling here if you were all right to begin with."

"Where's Dad?"

"I don't know."

"Why'd he leave? How come you don't know where he is? What happened? Tell me what happened."

"Well…he was upset."

"About…?"

"Is Keith okay?" Alice asked. "I mean, you haven't told him yet, have you?"

"He's sleeping. No, I haven't told him. What do you mean *yet*? I told you I wasn't ever going to tell him and—"

"Your father hasn't been over there, to your house, like tonight, has he?"

"No. Why? Tell me what's going on with you guys. Mom, you're scaring me."

"Maybe I should come over there. Maybe you and I should have a talk. Would you mind?"

"No. Come. Please. A…a talk would be good."

❦   ❦   ❦

Jessie was still awake, and more upset than ever now, an hour after the conversation she'd had with her mom on the porch. She wished she had another bowl of ice cream to pacify her, as the effects of her earlier one had worn off. She wished Ryan would've let her stay with him. It'd been cruel of him to cart her back home.

Her cell phone jingled, giving her a startle. She grabbed it off the nightstand. "Hello?"

"It's me," Ryan said.

"It's the middle of the night," Jessie exclaimed, lest he didn't realize it.

"So why aren't you sleeping?" he asked.

"Why aren't *you*?" she asked him back.

"Because guess who's sleeping in my bed?" Ryan said in a tone that sounded somewhere between anger and humor.

"That lawyer woman who was at your door the other day?"

"No! And Grace isn't a lawyer!"

"Grace?"

"She does have a name. Yes, Grace."

"She *looks* like a lawyer."

"Grandpa."

"Grandpa? He's there in your bed? What's he—"

"He just showed up here a while ago, with a suitcase, asking if he could spend the night."

"What happened?"

"I don't know. He wouldn't say, but he appears to be mad at Grandma."

"What's happening to this whole family?" Jessie snarled. "Everyone's going crazy."

"Yeah, I know. Anyway…I'm on the couch. I figured let the old guy have the bed. Thought I'd sneak in a call to you just so someone else knows his whereabouts."

"This is just too strange," Jessie said.

"Strange," Ryan agreed.

Jessie sighed. "What are we going to do, Ryan?"

She heard him sigh as well. "We're going to get some sleep now, kid, that's what. Talk to you tomorrow."

"It's already tomorrow."

"Later."

They said good night to one another and hung up. Jessie got out of bed and walked over to the dresser. She looked at the brown teddy bear sitting upon it. He seemed to be looking back at her as well. They were long-time buddies, she and he. He'd come to her by way of Santa when she was three years old. She picked him up, hugged him, and took him back to bed with her.

CHAPTER 12

❁

Keith missed Carla's presence in bed when he woke up. Seeing her side of the bed empty made his whole world feel empty. He laid his hand on her pillow, wishing he were touching her instead. It was strange that she'd risen before him this morning, when lately she'd been lingering in bed way longer. He wondered what was different about this morning. He wondered what was different about a lot of things lately. His wondering caused an ache in his gut.

He rolled out of bed to the smell of coffee reaching him all the way from the kitchen. It was tantalizing. He so needed some and couldn't wait to get downstairs and have a cup with Carla.

As Keith reached the bottom step, barefoot and shirtless, wearing only his white painter pants, he heard voices from the kitchen. When he got there he found his mother-in-law sitting at the table with Carla.

Alice gave him a casual smile, as if she were always there every day at this time of morning. "We're having coffee."

Keith took a mug out of the cupboard and poured himself some. It was the last of the pot, which told him this little coffee klatch had been in session for some time. "What's really going on?"

Carla shifted on her chair. "I couldn't sleep last night. I…I called to talk to Mom but—"

The phone rang. Keith answered it.

It was Nathan. "Alice there by any chance?"

Feeling like he was in the middle of a crazy dream, Keith glanced back at the table, at his mother-in-law, verifying her presence. "Uh…yeah…she is."

"Tell her I'm coming to get her."

Keith glanced out the side window. "Her car's in the driveway."

"Oh…uh, yeah, I suppose. Anyway I'm coming over."

Keith hung up in a stupor. "Nathan's on his way over. *Now* do you two wanna tell me what's going on?"

"Where was he calling from?" Alice asked.

Keith took a wild guess. "Home?"

"I doubt that," she said. "At least he wasn't there when I left."

Carla left the table and went about making a new pot of coffee. Keith watched her suspiciously.

"They had a little fight," she told him.

Keith looked at Alice. "You two never fight."

Alice didn't say anything, she just turned sadly quiet.

Keith sipped his coffee. The coffee maker on the counter was already sputtering and dripping fresh brew into the glass pot. Carla, in her robe and fussing about at nothing in particular now, looked weary, like the end of a day rather than the beginning.

He was just about to demand some serious answers when she put her head back and shouted toward the ceiling, "Jessie! Get a move on! The school bus will be here in minutes!"

It dawned on Keith that he hadn't heard anything from her room when he was up there. "I'll go check on her."

He left the kitchen and hurried upstairs. When he didn't get an answer to his knock on Jessie's door, he opened it and walked in. She wasn't there. He peered into the bathroom. She wasn't there either. This was one hell of a morning.

When he returned to the kitchen, Carla was just hanging up the phone. "Ryan called. She's at his place. She just now got there. He called to let us know right away."

Keith scratched his head. "Why would she go to Ryan's this early in the morning? What about school? And how come if you two were here in the kitchen you weren't aware of her leaving?"

"Oh, dear, that's so strange on top of everything else, isn't it?" Alice commented.

"Yeah," Keith agreed, without knowing the everything else. He closed his eyes and moaned. He felt like going back to bed and starting the day all over again. Maybe it would be normal the second time.

Carla was also puzzled, though made an assumption to the escape. "Jessie must have sneaked out the front way and then around to the back for her bike."

Keith studied his mother-in-law and his wife. Something was going on.

🍁　　🍁　　🍁

"You shouldn't have called Mom," Jessie scowled at her brother.

"You shouldn't have come over here," Ryan scowled back at her.

She put her backpack on the couch and sat down beside it, fixed to stay. "You shouldn't have called Mom."

"You shouldn't have run away."

"I didn't run away. I came here."

"Well, you shouldn't have and I had to let Mom know where you are."

"As if she'd miss me."

"She did. She was worried, glad I called."

"Well, for sure I'm not going back there. Ever."

"You're too young to leave home," her grandfather said, supporting himself against the wall as he put his shoes on and tied the laces.

"And you're too *old*," Ryan, in turn, told him. "Man…it's like this has become a home for wayward relatives. Excuse me…I have to get ready for work." He headed for the bathroom.

Jessie thought Nathan looked really rough, as if he hadn't slept a wink last night. She knew he'd spent the night here, but she didn't know why. "Why are you here and Grandma's at our house?"

"Why are *you* here?" he asked her back.

"Stuff is happening."

"Stuff," Nathan agreed.

Jessie figured he probably knew about her mother's infidelity, because likely her grandma would have told him. But was that reason for *him* to come stay with Ryan? She didn't get that. Somehow, by the look on his face, Jessie was starting to feel there was much more to worry about in this family than her mother's affair.

"Stuff," Nathan repeated. Ryan had come back into the room, and Nathan met his grandchildren's neediness for wanting to know more. "I…I don't know if you kids are old enough to handle this."

"I am," Ryan exclaimed. "Jessie can step out for a minute."

"I'm not leaving," she said. "I want to hear whatever there is to hear."

"You…the two of you…" Nathan began carefully, "you're not really my grandkids."

Ryan and Jessie's silence urged him to continue. "I just learned that your mom, Carla, well…she has a different biological father than me."

"What are you saying?" Jessie asked nervously.

"I *told* you you were too young," Ryan said.

Nathan sighed with a sadness so unlike him. "Your grandma, she was with another man way back then and…Carla's his child, not mine."

He didn't fill Ryan and Jessie's silence this time. He just let them absorb what he'd told them.

Eventually Jessie couldn't help remarking, "Guess it runs in the family."

Nathan gave a short laugh. "Yeah. Guess so. Anyway…I want you guys to know that I still love you no matter what. Okay?"

Ryan, still absorbing the shock of it, shook his head again and again and again. "Wow…"

"I'm a believer in truth," Nathan said, tucking his white painter shirt into the waist of his pants, "so there you have it."

"Why in our family?" Jessie protested.

Nathan sighed without an answer. "I'm going over to your house from here. Come on, I'll drop you at school on the way."

"I'm not going to school," she stated. "I'm quitting."

"No, you're not," Ryan said.

"I'll get a job at McDonald's or something."

"Not at thirteen you won't. Now do you ride with Grandpa or with me?"

As she stood there refusing to choose, Nathan impatiently opened the door to leave. "Get her there, Ryan. I gotta go. Thanks for letting me crash here last night. Jessie, mind your brother. See ya later."

Ryan rushed to the doorway, calling after him, "What'dya mean *later*? You coming back here? *Or what*?"

Jessie helped herself to a cookie from a bag on the kitchen counter.

Ryan marched toward her. "You can't do this, Jessie. I know you're upset, but you're going to school. I gotta leave for work and I'm dropping you there on my way."

"I'm too stressed to go to school."

"Life is tough, little sister. Deal with it."

"This family's a mess."

"If I don't get to work and you don't get to school, it'll be a worse mess. Come on, let's go." Ryan snatched her backpack off the couch and flung it at her.

"I'll go to school," she gave in, "but I'm coming here afterwards, not home."

"No."

"Please."

"No."

They started down the hallway together.

"One night?" Jessie pleaded.

Ryan didn't answer, but she would work on him as he drove her to school. She knew he would soften. He was a good brother.

❦   ❦   ❦

"What are you doing here?" Nathan demanded of Alice as he stormed into the Wade kitchen.

Alice dished it right back. "Why'd you take off last night? Where'd you go?"

Carla watched and listened to them with the responsibility of having caused their feud. This was so unreal, seeing her parents fight. And yet, before her very eyes, it was happening.

She handed her dad a mug of coffee. "Here, sit down and drink this."

Nathan took the coffee but stubbornly remained standing in the doorway.

"What happened between you two?" Keith asked his in-laws.

"You mean you haven't heard yet?" Nathan said, as if he were ready to spill the whole story of Carla's true father.

Carla herself had only learned about it last night. She hadn't a chance to tell Keith yet. Now wasn't a good time. "It's getting late," she said. "We've all got jobs to go to, right?"

"Heard what?" Keith asked.

"I don't have a job," Alice said with attitude, "I'm retired."

"Get in the truck," Nathan ordered her.

"Heard what?" Keith asked again.

"I've got my car," Alice sassed Nathan.

"Oh…yeah…well…then get in it and drive home."

"Do we still have one?" she asked. "A home?"

"Will somebody please tell me what's going on here?" Keith raised his voice over the commotion.

"We'll talk later," was the best Nathan could offer him.

Alice rose from her chair, gave Carla a good-bye hug, and followed Nathan out.

When they were gone, Keith questioned Carla with a silent look. When she went about gathering up the empty coffee mugs and putting them in the sink, purposely ignoring him, he gave up and left the kitchen to finish getting ready for work.

Carla felt relieved at being alone. At not being asked or told anything more for right now. She took deep breaths, relishing this moment that might very well be her only peaceful one of the day.

Carla dreaded opening the front door of Milo Printing and entering. But she'd walked out angrily yesterday and now she at least owed John a respectful resignation. Darcy glared at her from behind the counter.

As Carla silently walked toward John's office, Darcy let her know, "He's not in. Won't be in till noon today."

Carla stopped in her tracks. What a let down after the effort it took for her to even get this far.

"Want to leave him a message?" Darcy sneered.

Carla didn't answer. She just spun around and left.

On her way around the building to the back parking lot, Alonzo came rushing out the door from the lunchroom, calling, "Hey, Carla! Wait! I want to talk to you."

The desperation in his voice struck her like more trouble coming her way. She only wanted to get into her car and speed away.

But he reached her before she could even open the door and grabbed her by the arm. "Is it true you're quitting?"

Her saying nothing was as good as a yes.

Which Alonzo didn't want to accept. "You've been here a long time. Don't be hasty about this, Carla. Look, if this has anything at all to do about Friday night—"

"*If?*" she asked.

Though he looked sorry, his words were stupid. "Things happen at company parties."

Carla gave an unamused laugh. "Is that a man's point of view, *oh, well, things happen?*"

Alonzo cringed with regret. He wasn't being intentionally cruel, she knew that. It was probably just that he wasn't any better at handling this than she was. And then he bumbled on with, "I don't know what to say, except that I don't think you need to do this."

"But I do," Carla insisted.

"It's…not as bad as you make it to be."

She gave him a hateful look as she tried to explain what was going on inside of her. "I lost my best friend. I've made mockery of my job. My kids are ashamed of me. My parents are fighting because of me. I'm scared to death of losing my husband. And…and I'm thoroughly disgusted with myself."

Alonzo let go of her arm and stuck his hands in his pockets. "I'm sorry."

"Me too."

"What can I say? Do?"

"Are you a magician? No…I don't think you can fix this."

"Carla…" he started to say.

She held up a hand to stop him. Then she opened her car door and got in. They exchanged one more awkward look, then she drove away.

CHAPTER 13

❀

"So what was all that about?" Keith was anxious to ask Nathan as they carried their supplies from their trucks to the grounds of Tag Lake Park. Today's job was painting benches and picnic tables for the town. It looked like rain might be on the way, but if it came they also had some painting to do inside the recreation building.

"What was what about?" Nathan grumbled, his handsome seventy-year old face in a frown.

"Back there at my place, you and Alice, the two of you spending the night apart."

"Oh."

"Yeah, *oh*."

Nathan set his gallon can of green paint on the ground, squatted beside it, opened it, and mixed it with a stir stick. "You might say it was about trust."

"Trust?" Keith coaxed him on, opening his own can of green paint.

Nathan gave him the stir stick. "I believe in trust. Well, I *thought* I did. But come to find out…I've been a damn fool for believing in it."

"Yeah? How so?" Keith asked.

Nathan didn't answer. He chose a bench and began to work on it.

Keith stood in place watching him.

After vigorously going over it with a wire brush Nathan wiped it with a cloth, then began to apply some paint. The man was intensely into his work.

He'd only spread a couple of brush strokes when a dried leaf from last fall finally decided to abandon its tree and floated down directly onto the wet green. Annoyed, he picked it off and sputtered some cuss words.

While Keith couldn't help laughing, it failed to amuse Nathan.

Keith offered, "Guess we know what we're up against, painting in this tree-laden haven."

"It ain't fall. Leaves ain't supposed to be falling."

Another one drifted down but managed to miss the bench.

Keith got to work on the bench across the walk path from Nathan. "Okay, okay, why don't you just say what's really bugging you?"

"Nothing," Nathan snapped.

"Right, you're always this cheerful."

Nathan exchanged a look with Keith that seemed to re-evaluate their relationship enough to ask, "What would you do if your wife cheated on you?"

Keith's stomach did a flip. "What's this got to do with anything?"

"Answer my question."

"It's a stupid question."

Nathan shrugged. "So give me a stupid answer."

"Nothing. That's my answer, nothing." It was a stupid answer all right, Keith thought, because if Carla cheated on him he'd more likely do *something*. Sure, probably something drastic. But she never would, so he didn't need an actual answer. Jeez, where was Nathan coming from with this anyway?

Nathan picked a leaf out of his paint can. "Alice…she cheated on me."

Keith straightened back from his work, staring over at his father-in-law in dismay. "No."

"Yeah."

"Come on…" Keith looked for the truth, realizing it was indeed right there in Nathan's voice and eyes and everything that'd been going on that morning. "When?"

"Long time ago."

Keith thought ahead of speaking. "Well, you guys have a long past. Nobody's past is perfect. Don't dwell on something that—"

"Carla ain't my kid," Nathan said. "I just found out."

Keith's mouth dropped without words. He stood in a speechless stupor. Watching Nathan. Feeling sorry for Nathan. Feeling sorry for Carla. And for Alice. And for the whole world that could get so complex sometimes.

Nathan laid his brush across the top of his paint can and sat down in the grass with a sigh. "Alice had an affair, way back then, with my best friend, no less."

Keith shook his head at it.

Though Nathan also shook his head, he said, "Yeah, my little Alice, beholder of truth and goodness. You can't imagine what this has done to me. My whole life…it's suddenly not the way I thought it was all along."

"How come this happened to come up now all of a sudden, after all these years?"

Nathan dropped eye contact with Keith as he said, "It's Carla's fault."

"What do you mean, Carla's fault?" Keith asked excitedly.

"Nothing."

"Damn it, Nathan! You can't just say something like that then tell me it's nothing!"

A little boy of about four and his mother, coming along the walk path, were both startled by Keith's outburst. The woman hurried the child along, as if to safety.

"Are you guys painting?" the boy managed to ask the men in his hasty passing.

"We're on a break," Nathan responded. And then motioning at Keith, he jeered, "My boss here likes to yell at me."

The woman gave Keith a nasty look and a piece of her mind. "You get much more out of people when you're civil to them!"

"Thanks," Keith scoffed at Nathan when they were alone again.

"You're welcome," Nathan said, enlightened by his own quick wit.

Thinking again about Alice's coming over to talk with Carla in the middle of the night, Keith could now interpret it as, "So Carla knows."

"She does now, yes."

"And…?"

Nathan shrugged. "Guess it doesn't seem to matter a whole lot to her, from what Alice says."

"Nor should it to you," Keith advised him. "You and Carla…you're still father and daughter, no matter what."

As Nathan got to his feet, ready to resume his painting, Keith gave him a sympathetic pat on the back. "I know how you must be feeling, the shock of it and all, but—"

"No, you don't know! *Do you*?"

"No, I suppose not," Keith corrected himself.

"Sorry," Nathan apologized. He dipped his brush into the paint and made another start on his bench.

Keith stood doing nothing for the next few minutes. He felt upset. Surely no where near as upset as Nathan was feeling…but something…just something beneath the surface of it all…was giving him a very queasy feeling.

Keith took a long look at the sky. It was dreary. An exact match to the way he was feeling. Though he'd totally lost his energy, his job commanded him to work. There was very little talk between him and Nathan from then on. Which was probably for the best.

🍁 🍁 🍁

Carla drove to the Tag Lake Park at noon looking for her father and Keith. She parked her car beside their trucks in the parking lot and walked across the grass toward the picnic table where she spotted them.

"Well, look who's here," Keith greeted her approach with surprise.

They were eating their lunch. She'd caught them at a good time. She smiled, said hi, and then directed her attention solely onto her father. Or at least onto the only man she'd ever known to be her father for almost forty years. In one sense he seemed so different to her now, yet in another sense no different at all. "Are you okay?" she asked him.

He said nothing, but the glisten in his eyes expressed his hard-felt emotions.

"He's not doing too well," Keith told her. "How *you* doing?"

With that, Carla determined that Keith knew. Well…about her and her dad, anyway. But did he also know about her and Alonzo? Maybe her dad told him. He'd threatened to. She stood sickened with the sudden onset of finding that she maybe had much more to deal with here than she'd expected.

As if Nathan read her concern and singled it out, he said, "Keith knows about your not being my daughter. We talked."

Carla sat down beside him on the bench. "But you *are* my father."

Nathan gave her a look, but didn't really see what she wanted him to see. "You know what," he concluded, "I guess one's never too old to learn that things aren't always as they seem. You never know when the truth's going to come slamming down on you, making a mockery out of all you believed in."

It hurt Carla that he considered her a mockery. It wasn't her fault that she was conceived from her mother's one-night stand. It *was* her fault, however, that she herself recently had a one-night stand outside of her own marriage, and because of that her mom felt that telling Nathan about her own past might stop him from telling Keith about that Friday night.

Carla looked over at Keith, who was looking strangely back at her. She still worried that maybe he did know about her and Alonzo. *Did he?* Or did he really only know about her mother and her biological father? Everything was so mixed up, messed up. Life had been so sweet and simple only a short time back. She missed her old life…where Keith was her one and only man, and her father was her one and only father.

Suddenly Nathan got up from the picnic table and, without a word, walked away. It only took Carla a moment to know that she had to go after him.

He was walking so fast she had to run to catch him. When she did, she grabbed him by the arm and made him stop. He hung his head, unable to look at her.

"You *are* my dad," she insisted. "You always have been and always will be. Don't put up a wall between us. You don't have to do that. I don't *want* you to do that. You're my dad. I need you to be my dad."

Nathan's eyes slowly met again with hers. But they were still full of doubt. "A lot has changed, sweetheart. For me as well as for you."

"No, not really, don't say that."

"I'm not just talking about the relationships of you and me, and your mom and me. I'm also referring to you and Keith. To what's happened, or happening, there."

Carla looked back over her shoulder at Keith, still sitting at the table.

"You haven't told him yet, have you?" Nathan assumed.

"No," she said.

"When?"

"Never."

Nathan sighed. "Carla, you have to. Being up front is the only way to go with this. Look what happened with your mother and me. All that time with such a lie between us, and now—"

"It's my fault," she owned the blame. "Because of what I did, it brought out this problem between you and Mom. I am so sorry."

"Carla…" Nathan said, placing his hands on her shoulders, seeming more sad than angry, "how could you have lowered yourself like that?"

She looked away from him in shame.

"I thought you loved Keith," Nathan said.

"I do," she said without hesitance or doubt. "It had nothing to do with Keith. It's like Mom, she always loved you. She told me about…well, what happened back then. And how she never wanted to hurt you over her wrong doing. Just like I never wanted to hurt Keith over what I did."

Nathan shook his head. "It's all about truth, Carly. Don't you get it? A husband and wife have to be honest with each other. There's no other way."

"People make mistakes, Dad."

"There's no other way," he repeated.

"There has to be."

"People admit to them and pay for them. *Right up front.* They don't hide them until they grow into something much bigger and darker down the line."

"That's a chance I have to take."

"Keith is a forgiving person, not a stupid one. Give him some credit."

Carla shifted from foot to foot.

"For God's sake, Carla!" Nathan bellowed. "Maybe I just might think a lot more of Keith than you do, because I won't let him unknowingly go along with something happening behind his back that he deserves to know about."

"No!" Carla argued. "You can't tell him. It's not your business, not your place and—"

"What's going on over here?" Keith was coming toward them with a look of concern.

"Nothing," Carla responded quickly enough to sound more doubtful than sure.

"Just a little father-daughter spat," Nathan explained. Then added through a grin, "Which I guess proves we're still officially father and daughter. Right, Carla?"

His statement, along with the hug he gave her, made Carla feel better. She hoped it also meant that she could count on him to not tell Keith about Alonzo.

Keith was smiling over the rectified father-daughter connection. And then he was next to hug Carla. And then before she could no longer hold back a gush of tears, she said she had to leave and hurried off toward the parking lot.

Keith thought he understood her urgency and called after her, "Yeah, I'm sure you're on your lunch break, too."

Only when she was opening the door to her car did she announce back to the guys, "I don't have a job anymore. I quit."

She left the two of them standing in awe. There would definitely be some explaining to do later, but maybe by later she'd come up with some way of doing that.

Delany's Deli wasn't crowded by any means. Carla sat in a booth. Eating a bowl of split pea soup, she felt that everyone there was watching her and judging her. Such as the couple across from her, frequently turning their faces toward her and raising their eyebrows suspiciously. And the guy at the counter, who kept sneaking looks at her. And an old bearded man, with his cane resting against his table, studying her as if she were someone to be pitied. Even the waitress, when she'd taken her order, seemed infatuated with her presence.

Carla felt as self-conscious as if she were wearing a sign on her forehead reading, *unfaithful and illegitimate*. As if everyone knew her from the inside out, better than she knew herself.

She tried focusing on the view out the window beside her. It was raining. A light mist had only just started when she'd left her dad and Keith in the park, but now it was coming down hard. Splashing against the sidewalk, mirroring car headlights on the street, dimming the whole natural spirit of the day.

Anyway the pea soup was hot and nourishing and soothing. Okay, that was helping. The little table candle, flickering cozily before her, felt equally nice and helpful. The next song coming from the ceiling speakers was not, however, in the least bit fair. Neil Diamond's *Play Me* placed her right back to Friday night, dancing in Alonzo's arms, kissing Alonzo, getting lost with Alonzo.

Her good/bad trance was suddenly interrupted by the waitress speaking to her. "W-what…?" Carla had to ask.

"Can I get you anything else?" the waitress evidently repeated herself.

Carla shook her head. "Uh…oh…no thank you. I'm fine."

The waitress put the check on the table and left.

The song was over, the soup was gone, and Carla felt so very alone. Scared. Lost. Sad. Sorry.

"People like you ought to be locked up," said an old woman, stopping beside Carla's booth.

Carla looked up. There, with straggly white hair, sunken eyes, a toothless mouth, and a black shawl, stood a witch. One more eerie than any Halloween might've ever fabricated.

"Excuse me?" Carla asked, immediately guilty of sin and amazed at her approached punishment.

The woman started to sputter more words but was interrupted by the man who came along behind her and took her by the arm. "Let's go now, Mother. Let's not bother this nice lady."

The *witch* resisted her son and continued to threaten Carla. "You'll pay for what you did, I tell you. And you—"

"I'm sorry," the man worked in an apology. "She's very mixed up. She thinks you're the person who stole her purse from her in a similar restaurant a long time ago. She's got this past experience locked in her head. Forgive her, please."

Carla nodded and the man took his mother away. Relieved as Carla was, it left her with a haunting after affect.

She again stared out the window at the gloomy afternoon that so matched her heart. She wished that her only crime had merely been, in fact, stealing a purse from an old lady rather than having cheated on her husband.

How she missed her life as it used to be, just last week before her mistake. She wished she could go back and undo her incident with Alonzo. It shouldn't have happened. She didn't understand why it did. She needed comforting so badly. She needed Keith's comfort but didn't deserve it. There was no one she could be close to, regarding this.

A crazy thought suddenly entered Carla's mind. Like maybe the person she really needed to talk to, to get past all of this, was Alonzo. She sighed, overwhelmed at the feeling of new guilt that came with a solution that could only be worse than its cause. She continued watching the raindrops roll down the window, weighing her thoughts very cautiously.

Carla cringed when Keith came into the kitchen after work that evening, spurting, "Okay, so let's hear about why you quit your job today."

It wasn't that she hadn't expected the subject she'd briefly dumped on him earlier to continue tonight, it was more that she still wasn't ready. But he was, and she'd better be.

Carla forked the pork chops over in the frying pan and gave a casual shrug. "I'd had enough, that's all."

"Enough?" Keith didn't understand. Of course he didn't. She'd always expressed how much she loved her job.

Carla put down the fork and turned to face him. "Guess I just need a change."

"You hate change."

"*The* change, that's for sure."

He smiled apologetically. "Sorry about labeling you with menopause, but lately you—"

"I know. I understand. I admit I've been a little moody."

"A *little*?" he exclaimed through a grin. "When you showed up at the park today, I knew that it was bothering you about Nathan not being your biological father. He'd told me about that, and that's a tough one. But as you left the park, you announced that you quit your job and I *didn't* get that."

Carla dropped eye contact with him. She'd already stated that she'd quit because she needed a change, but he obviously wasn't going to let her off that easily. She wasn't ready with another reason, a better reason, the true reason.

Keith put his hands on her shoulders and said reassuringly, "Hey…honey…it's okay…I mean, I'm okay with your quitting your job if that's what you want. I…I just want to know that…that you're okay, that's all. *Are* you?"

"Yes."

"Really?"

"Yes. No. I don't know."

Keith laughed softly, then drew her closer for a hug. She was glad he was taking her evasiveness so well. She wished she were taking it as well herself. She cherished this moment in his arms. As long as she didn't have to explain herself, the world seemed okay.

The smell of burning pork chops eventually interrupted their intimate interlude.

"Oh no!" she cried, turning to the stove, turning off the burner, shoving the pan aside.

It was too late. The meat was ruined.

Keith, bless him, said, "It's okay. You know I like 'em well done. I'll open a window."

Carla was on the verge of tears. Not because of the burnt pork chops. Not because of the news about her father. Not because she'd just quit her job. The main thing…the very main thing bothering her was that she'd cheated on Keith. And his sweetness toward her intensified her guilt. *Oh, the guilt.*

Keith came back from the window and took her into his arms again. "Nathan's still your father, whether by blood or by gosh. And we're financially okay for you not to work, if that's what you really want. And the pork chops are fine, honey…really."

A helpless laugh escaped Carla, which helped her feel better. Then she and Keith exchanged a passionate kiss that also worked well for her.

"As a matter of fact," Keith said, getting a beer out of the fridge, "I think Jessie likes her meat well done too, doesn't she?"

"She won't be home tonight," Carla had to tell him. "She…well, Ryan called and said she's going to stay with him for a night…or so."

"Oh yeah, why's that?"

"Who knows," Carla dismissed it lightly. "Teenagers, huh?"

"Unpredictable," Keith agreed. "Just like my wife. Okay…well…so it's just you and me, kid, right?"

Carla was filled with gratitude for his good nature. "You're wonderful, you know?"

He grinned. "Yeah, I know."

CHAPTER 14

Things were relatively calm over the next two weeks, though not especially in a good way. Carla avoided getting into anything more with her parents, to the point of barely speaking with them now. Nathan took up regular residency with Ryan, as did Jessie who stretched her *one night or so* into much longer. Poor Ryan, a young man wanting to be out on his own and then his family one by one starts invading him. Carla understood that Nathan got the bed, Jessie the couch and Ryan his sleeping bag on the floor. Sunday family dinners were discontinued, and Alice became somewhat of a recluse.

Carla managed to have a heart to heart talk with John Milo, and it was only with sad reluctance that he accepted her resignation. Keith was amazingly good-natured about so many things he didn't fully understand, it almost seemed like he really didn't care one way or another what might be behind any of them. And Carla had fallen into the rut of having become way too accustomed to being a homebody.

The time came for her to look for another job. She had to get out and make a new life for herself, despite her depression. It wouldn't be easy finding new employment in Tag Lake. Maybe she'd have to settle for cashiering at a supermarket or a gas station. No job would ever compare to how good she'd had it at Milo Printing before…Oh, how she'd messed up her life because of one night's mistake, not to mention how she'd messed up the lives of her whole family. Oh, the guilt that she carried continually.

She wondered if Alonzo's life had become anywhere near as messed up as hers because of that night. It was strange how she was beginning to think about him differently lately. Like in some strange way she thought it might be easier to talk to him right now than to Keith.

Well, she needed to talk with *someone*, that was for sure. She was becoming so emotionally filled up with hurtful things left unsaid and undealt with that it seemed like time was certainly making matters worse rather than better.

One morning, after a fourth cup of coffee and slamming the Tag Lake newspaper classifieds back down on the kitchen table, Carla went to the phone and dialed Milo Printing. Darcy answered.

"May I speak to Alonzo Quinn, please?" Carla asked, disguising her voice.

Alonzo answered the transfer with surprise, as he didn't get many personally directed calls. He was even more surprised finding it was Carla.

She nervously asked if he would meet her for lunch. And he nervously said okay.

They met at a bar and grill on the southern outskirts of town. Carla, in jeans and a pink tee-shirt, was waiting in a booth when he got there. He sat down across the table from her, a scared smile on his face, questions burning in his eyes.

"Don't get the wrong idea about this," Carla began. "It's just…I'm feeling very alone these days and…and I just don't know where to turn."

"So you turned to me," he said.

"You wrecked my life, Alonzo."

The waitress approached, overhearing Carla's statement but pretending she didn't. "You two ready to order?" she asked.

"Grilled cheese sandwich and coffee," Alonzo said.

The waitress jotted it on her pad then looked at Carla.

When Carla froze from deciding or even speaking, Alonzo told the waitress, "Same for her."

"Sorry," Carla apologized to him after the waitress left. "My brain's not working very well these days." She eased up enough to give him a little thank-you smile. "I'm amazed that you ordered my absolute favorite sandwich."

"I know a grilled-cheese girl when I see her."

Carla started to relax.

"So…" Alonzo said, "I wrecked your life, huh?"

She regretted how bluntly she'd charged him with that a minute ago. "I, uh…"

"It takes two to tango, y'know," he said almost as bluntly.

On her way by, the waitress paused to ask them, "Everything all right here?"

Alonzo gave a nod and she left.

A quietness came between Carla and and him. It was awkward, suddenly not having anything more to say to one another. Carla filled the time by playing with the little silver heart that hung from a silver chain around her neck.

"That's nice," Alonzo finally said in observance of it.

"It's from my husband."

Alonzo nodded, then found the time fitting to say, "Look, I'm sorry about that night, but I can't take it back. Neither of us can. We can only go forth now."

Sitting there face to face with Alonzo, Carla wasn't entirely sure now that he was the right one for her to be talking to. "Easy for you to say…you don't have a spouse and a family and…*do you*?"

He laughed. "No. But I'm human, y'know, and it does bother me that it's left this sort of effect on you." He shifted in his seat. "So what do you want me to do at this point, Carla?"

Now that he'd actually asked, she was caught without an answer. She shrugged and gave him a sheepish look.

Alonzo reached across the table for her hand, held it gently, and used his dark Latin eyes on her much like he had that night. "To be honest, I'm not sorry about what happened between you and me. I'm only sorry you got hurt by it."

"That's a two-sided comment," she said.

"Yeah, I guess. Truth is, I was very attracted to you. And the opportunity unfolded. And—"

"Did you take advantage of me because I'd had too much to drink?"

Alonzo laughed.

His amusement offended Carla. She frowned at him.

When the waitress brought their sandwiches and coffee, she again observed her guests curiously but didn't question them this time.

When she left, Carla confronted Alonzo with annoyance. "You think it's funny that I got a bit over indulged that night?"

He nodded, laughed some more, and picked up half of his sandwich. "Yeah. And you will too, Carla, when I tell you why. Those drinks you were having, Marty's specials, they—"

"How could he do that to me?" she protested. "He made it so easy for me to keep drinking them and—"

"Carla, Carla…" Alonzo stopped her, "there was no booze in those drinks Marty made for you."

"What?"

"They were perfectly harmless. He knew you weren't a drinker and he respected that and mixed you up something that…well, tasted rather risqué, I guess…but, no, your drinks were strictly non-alcoholic."

"H-how do you know?"

"We talked, he and I, since then."

"And you believed him?"

"Yeah."

"But…but I had a hangover the next morning," Carla said.

"I'm sure you were just filled with remorse over having had sex with me and not from anything you drank. Or *thought* you drank."

"But I felt and behaved so different that night. The drinks, they—"

"Funny how that works. Sometimes when people *think* they've drunk something intoxicating, but really hadn't, they get the same reaction as if they had."

"No."

Alonzo laughed. "Yes. Now eat your sandwich." He took a bite of his.

Carla wasn't hungry. She was insulted over having been had. And disturbed to a new degree over her mistake. "So you mean I…I had sex with you without even being under the influence."

"That's right." Alonzo said with his mouth full. "And now that's going to bother you even more, isn't it?"

"I…I've got nothing to blame my…my behavior on."

"Except that maybe you were just as attracted to me as I was to you. Could that honestly be, Carla? The only way you can possibly deal with any of this is to be honest."

She stared at her untouched sandwich. This certainly was a whole new shock wave she hadn't expected. She should never have asked Alonzo to meet her for lunch. She felt stupid, finding that on top of everything else she'd been had by Marty. And that she'd been totally sober when she'd had sex with Alonzo. She was a worse person than she'd already believed herself to be.

She kept quiet, allowing Alonzo to finish his sandwich. Then he wiped his mouth with his napkin, gazed at the wall clock, and said, "I'm going to have to get back to work."

Carla started to get some money out for the check, but he wanted to take care of it. He left a tip on the table, and she followed him to the front of the restaurant. She waited while he paid the cashier, then together they walked out to their cars in the parking lot.

Oh, how different things were now. Worse, not better. She couldn't blame drinking for her behavior that night. She'd lost her only excuse. Having no excuse intensified her shame.

"Come back to Milo," Alonzo said carefully and sincerely as they stood at their cars. "We need you there. Marty's sorry for the joke he pulled on you. Everybody knows what happened that night, thanks to Darcy, but nobody's making wise cracks about it. And Darcy…well, Darcy is Darcy. Everybody's got her figured. Everybody likes you a whole lot more than her, Carla, believe me. Come back."

She shook her head and opened her car door. "No."

"Call me any time then, okay? I don't know if there's anything I can say or do to help you, but I'll sure try. Really."

She nodded, got in her car, and drove off.

That night as Carla strolled into the living room where Keith sat reading in his favorite chair, he didn't even look up. He'd been quiet at supper and since supper, just as she'd been. It wasn't a relaxing sort of quiet.

It was a long while before he put his book down and acknowledged her presence.

Then patting his knee, he beckoned her over to him with, "Hey…"

She went to sit on his lap, feeling like a child about to confess something awful to her father. Though there could be nothing worse than a wife confessing to her husband that she'd cheated on him. She still didn't want to tell Keith, but she had to. She couldn't go on trying to hide it from him, keeping it bottled up inside of her. As it was, difficult things left unsaid didn't go away but rather only festered.

"What's wrong?" he asked, easily sensing that there was something.

"Just hold me," she said.

His arms tightened around her. It made her feel safe. It made her feel like talk was unnecessary, and closeness the best communication there could be.

Until he prompted her with, "What, Carla, what?"

"Nothing."

"It doesn't seem like nothing to me."

She shrugged, smiled her way out of it, got off his lap, and left him only with an apologetic kiss on his forehead. "I just needed to…well, I mean it's been like a long time that I…well, you know…that I told you I love you. I just wanted you to know that I do."

He smiled and told her he loved her, too.

The phone rang, and Keith left for the kitchen to get it. Carla followed him. After answering hello, he handed it to her. "It's Darcy."

Carla's hand trembled as she put the phone to her ear.

As soon as she said hello, Darcy bellowed, "Have you told him yet?"

Carla knew exactly what she meant. And when she didn't answer, Darcy knew exactly what *that* meant.

"Put Keith back on the phone," Darcy said to Carla's silence.

"No," Carla responded.

"I'm coming over."

"No, don't. Why are you doing this? I left Milo, isn't that enough?"

Darcy laughed wickedly.

"Leave me alone," Carla pleaded desperately, despite Keith's being right there listening. She had to be more careful, with her words and her tone. She pretended the call was related to some tickets. "Thanks for calling, Darcy, but, uh…please don't bug me any more about those tickets. I'm not interested."

"I care about Keith and it bothers me that he doesn't—"

"I *know* what you care about," Carla said.

"I'm coming over."

"No! Wait! Please!"

Darcy hung up and Carla was left holding a dead phone. When she lowered it from her ear, Keith came to take it from her and hang it up. His trying to read into the situation on his own allowed her some time. Time with which she didn't know what to do with except to just stand there blankly.

When she found her voice, she told him, "We need to talk."

Chapter 15

Rain had been falling outside for the past hour, and the house had become chilly and damp. When Keith lit the living-room fireplace, it quickly radiated a comforting warmth.

He sat down on the floor before it with Carla and put an arm around her. "Better?"

Though she nodded, he doubted that she was. She'd had a troubled spirit all evening, but especially since Darcy's phone call a while ago. A phone call after which she'd seriously decided she had something to talk to him about. Something that was obviously not good.

Keith allowed her the time she seemed to need. They sat cuddled together, watching the red and yellow flames dance amongst the logs. The setting seemed almost too romantic to fill with conversation. Especially if it were to be a bad one.

But when Carla was ready, she began with, "It's about that Friday night."

Keith's worry lessened. "This is what's been eating at you so?"

"I never wanted to choose going to Milo's event over Jessie's play that night, but it was mandatory."

"I know. And Jessie knows. Aren't you convinced by now that we're okay with that?"

Carla couldn't let it go. "That night…oh, Keith…I'm so sorry."

"It's okay, it's okay." He tightened his hold of her.

"There's more," she said, as if there were yet a mountain to climb. "The meeting…it was also a celebration, you know, and—"

"Yeah, I know."

"There was drinking at the party."

Keith grinned at her confession. "You're telling me you actually had something to drink?"

The solemnity possessing her made him further evaluate, "You had a *lot* to drink?"

She was wrestling hard with her thoughts. And out of them came, "I was with another man that night."

Keith shrugged, stupidly assessing, "Milo consists of all men except for you and Darcy, right?"

"I had sex with one of them. There. After the party. After everyone else left. He and I—"

"*What?*" Keith's brain felt like a car screeching to a sudden stop.

"I didn't mean to."

Keith got up from the floor, repeating himself, "*What?*"

"Oh, Keith…God, I didn't mean to." Carla also got to her feet, quickly stepping around behind a chair, as if she were taking cover from him. As if she were scared of him. Maybe she should be.

"What guy?" Keith wanted, *and didn't want*, to know.

"One of the employees. He and—"

"A name."

"Alonzo. He…well…I know there's no excuse, but it…it just sort of happened."

Keith's shoulders drooped from the emotional weight bearing down on him. This wasn't Carla. Not his Carla. She really wasn't telling him what he thought he heard, was she? "You…had sex with him?" he sought further verification.

She gave a slow nod. "And I've been living with the shame and guilt of it ever since. And…and Darcy has turned against me because—"

"What's *she* got to do with this?" Keith shouted.

Carla cowered, as if she expected him to hit her. But Keith stayed on his side of the chair. He'd never struck his wife. He never would. He hated that she looked so threatened by him now. She didn't need to be. He only had to know, "Why?"

"There is no why," she said.

"There has to be," he insisted. "You're wrong about it just sort of happening, because those sort of things don't *just happen*. Tell me why, Carla. What's been so bad for you here, with me, that you—"

Keith ran his fingers through his hair, containing his inner emotions that wanted to howl or throw something or break something. Instead he sank down on the couch and buried his face in his hands.

After a few minutes, Carla came to sit beside him. "I'm sorry."

"This can't be us…" he murmured, "it just can't be."

She put her hand on his leg. "I know."

"I don't know where I'm at right now, and I guess I sure as heck don't know where *you're* at. Why, Carla? If I just knew why. That phone call from Darcy…what does she possibly have to do with this?"

"She'd been interested in Alonzo. Which I didn't know until after…Well, she felt betrayed by me."

"Yeah…" Keith related.

"She turned against me after that, as if I'd purposely set out to torment her. And she made things so difficult for me at Milo because of it that I felt pressured into quitting. And…and now she's been threatening to tell you if I didn't and—"

"You weren't going to tell me if she hadn't *pressured* you?" Keith saw Carla's confession from a whole different angle.

"I…I didn't like keeping it from you, but I also didn't like the idea of telling you. I didn't know which was worse, which would hurt you the worst."

"Worst?" Keith exclaimed. "You don't think that your doing it in the first place, rather than telling or not telling me about it, was the worst?"

Carla said nothing. Which felt to Keith like still another worst in this. "Your dad…your parents…they know about this?"

"Yes."

"What about Jessie?"

"Both she and Ryan know."

Keith moaned. "Christ, Carla…I'm the last to know?"

The way she sat looking at him through tearing eyes made him feel that he was the bad one here. He felt sympathetic, and more concerned over her feelings than over his own right now. He put his arms around her and held her. She was shivering despite the heat from the fireplace.

"It's okay," he said. "We'll be okay."

After a few minutes, he suggested to her, "Go up to bed. I'll be there soon."

Keith picked up his book, stared at it, then slammed it back down on the table. He doubted that he'd ever get back to finishing it now. He doubted that he'd ever get the picture out of his mind of Carla having sex with another man. He felt sick, ten times worse than when he'd had the flu last winter. There was a rage inside of him that wanted to burst out of him like a crazy man. But he wouldn't let it. No. When he was truly calm, he'd join Carla upstairs.

The front doorbell rang, startling him out of his deep dejection. Before he could get there, it rang over and over incessantly.

He opened the door and a rain-wet Darcy came charging in past him. He closed the door and followed her into the living room.

When she reached the center of the room, she spun around announcing, "I'm here because I'm your friend and there's something I need to tell you."

Keith didn't like her attitude. Or for that matter *her*. "First of all, Darcy, you and I, we aren't friends. Maybe you were, and I say *were*, friends with Carla. But you and I…we never were. Second of all, you don't need to tell me something that I already know."

Darcy's mouth dropped. She wasn't used to being shot down ahead of her say. "You *know*? That your quiet little do-gooder wife screwed a coworker?"

"How poetic you make that sound," Keith scoffed. "Yes, I know. And I also know how you deserted her after her mistake."

"Mistake? You call what she did a *mistake*?"

Keith pointed to the door. "You can leave now."

Darcy stayed put. "Carla wasn't going to tell you. She was going to keep her dirty little *mistake* a secret from you. But I thought you deserved a lot more consideration than that."

"*Did* you?"

Darcy sneered with a witch's pleasure. "So when *did* she tell you? Tonight, following my phone call? Well, you can thank me that you know the truth now."

"I'll thank you to leave, that's all."

Darcy wasn't ready to leave. "I always thought Carla had the perfect life. I envied her, you know? And I was hoping to make as much out of my own life. I was hoping that Alonzo might be the right guy for me. But no…little miss has-to-have-it-all steps into the way of—"

"Don't blame Carla for your own failures, Darcy."

"She's not the angel you think she is."

Keith felt his blood pressure rising in sync with his voice. "Why are you so interested in coming between Carla and me?"

"I'm not," Darcy snapped.

Keith argued it with a certainty he'd felt long before now. "I don't think you care about what went on between Carla and Alonzo as much as you care about what goes on between Carla and me. Isn't that right?"

He took Darcy's non-answer as a yes.

She'd come onto him several times over the years behind Carla's back. She, Carla's supposed best friend. Keith had always sloughed it off like it was nothing. Certainly nothing he ever needed to tell Carla about. But he'd had enough of Darcy's repulsiveness. "It isn't enough that you messed up your own marriage? You have to try and wreck ours as well?"

"You don't know anything about Bill and me."

"You forgot that I knew Bill. And had many talks with Bill."

Darcy's painted face dimmed.

Keith pointed to the door. "Leave!"

"You are so stupid, Keith! Carla doesn't appreciate you."

"And I don't appreciate *you*. Leave!"

"You're just as blind as she is."

"What goes on between Carla and me is our business, not yours."

"And what about all the times you looked at me like you wondered what it would be like having me instead of her? Who's business should that be?"

"Talk about blind…boy, did you misread those looks."

"I don't think so," she said, coming toward him rather than the door, much like a black widow spider coming to attack her prey.

Keith held up a stop hand. "You're crazy! Get the hell out of here! Now!"

"I could soothe your wounded heart real nice, Keith," she said, pathetically.

"You're out of your freakin' mind!" He grabbed her wrist and pulled her all the way to the door. He opened it and shoved her out. "Don't ever come back here. Or call here. Or use either Carla's name or my name in anything you say."

Darcy's last look upon him was a sneer, as if she felt she'd won her fight after all. Then she left the stoop and ran through the rain to her car.

Keith slammed the door shut.

When he got upstairs he found Carla just standing in the middle of the bedroom in her nightshirt. Looking sad and lost. He took her in his arms and held her. Nothing more needed to be said. For now.

🍁 🍁 🍁

They watched TV together, the three of them. Jessie sitting cross-legged on the floor, Ryan on a kitchen stool, and Nathan claiming ownership of the entire couch in his comfortable sprawl.

"You need to get more furniture," Jessie told her brother.

"Or less company," he said, with a crooked grin.

"Good couch," Nathan remarked.

"Try sleeping on it," Ryan said. Then asked, "How long you planning to stay here anyway?"

"Don't know."

"So…how's Grandma doing?"

"Don't know."

"I want to know what our whole family's going to do about all of this," Jessie firmly stated.

"Do?" Ryan asked, with the return of his grin.

His coolness irritated her. She got up off the floor and marched around the small room. "About Mom and Dad. And Grandma and Grandpa. And…and you and Grace."

Now Ryan outwardly laughed at her. "Okay, saver of the world…why don't you come up with one solution that fits all."

"You're so smug," she snarled.

"I think he gets it from you," Nathan joked.

Jessie turned her fire on him. "I think you should forgive Grandma and go back to her."

"You do, huh? Well, how about you go home and forgive your mother?"

It was a totally different situation, and Jessie resented his comparison. She turned to Ryan. "What do you see in that *older woman* that you can't find in a girl your own age?"

"None of your business," he said.

She threw up her hands. "That's the problem with this family. Nobody's nobody else's business. We're all just spinning around on our own."

"Huh?" Nathan sat up, squinting with confusion.

"Jessie, listen to yourself," Ryan told her. "Aren't you actually telling yourself to go home and do your own part in keeping the family ties intact?"

He was right, Jessie admitted in the privacy of her mind. She was stupidly saying one thing and doing another. A sure sign of immaturity. She hated that she was but thirteen. Hated that she wasn't handling this better.

"All right…all right…" Nathan got off the couch and came to give her a hug. "Right now we're all in a hellova mess. But it'll get better again."

"When?" Jessie, in the tight wrap of his arms, could only ask.

Her grandpa didn't say. And when she exchanged a look with Ryan, he merely shook his head and shrugged. So much for maturity. The so-called mature ones in this room were only *pretending* to be mature. Actually, they were no wiser than she. And somehow…that made her feel just a little better.

CHAPTER 16

After Keith left for work the next morning Carla took a cup of coffee out onto the porch and sat in the swing. She was supposed to be feeling better for having told him about her and Alonzo, but she was feeling worse. Why was she feeling worse when Keith had taken it so well?

He'd been upset at first. Then pretty riled at Darcy's visit. But after Darcy left, he came upstairs and held Carla with the sweetest and most tender regard. And then he'd held her in his arms most of the night as they'd slept. How could she possibly want anything more from him?

She sipped her hot coffee, listening to the birds chirping in nearby trees. It was a beautiful morning. Spring was her favorite season. It meant the coming of new life, new hope, enlightenment. Exactly the things she needed. She'd made an awful mistake that she couldn't take back, but maybe spring would at least open the way for her to go forward again.

Except...right now she couldn't stop wondering if Keith's tolerance of what she'd done actually showed how much he loved her or how much he didn't love her. What were his true sentiments? She didn't feel like she knew. She was his wife, she should know. Or could it be that she was no longer worthy of sharing them, no matter what they were? Had she lost that right? She now had to worry as much about what was going on inside of Keith's head as she did of what was going on inside of hers. She missed the simplicity of what her life was about before that Friday night. It was tough, realizing that it might never be like that again.

When she'd finished her coffee and had thought her thoughts over and over until she couldn't think at all anymore, Carla left the swing and went back into the house. She sat at the kitchen table with the newspaper classifieds. She went up and down the columns with a red pen, looking for job possibilities but finding none. Eventually she crumpled the newspaper into a ball.

She needed to talk to someone. But who was left in her life that...

Mike! The idea of calling her brother in San Francisco newly inspired her. She did after all have somebody left to turn to. She went to the phone and dialed his number.

"Yeah...?" came a groggy voice.

Carla swallowed hard then spoke with a smile, "Mike...it's Carla."

"Carla...hey...what's the emergency?"

"Oh...the time difference," she realized. "I woke you. Sorry."

He laughed good-naturedly. "That's okay. My alarm was going to go off in another hour anyway. What's up?"

"I need to talk to you about something, Mike, or I'll go crazy."

"Don't do that. I'm here."

"I cheated on Keith."

"*What*?" Mike screeched.

"I didn't mean to. It was a stupid mistake that just happened and I've been miserable ever since."

"I should think so."

"I'm really having trouble getting over the guilt and—"

"Does Keith know?"

"Yes. Everyone knows. Including you now. And I was hoping I'd feel better after talking with you."

There was a discomforting pause before Mike belted out, "What's the matter with you, Carla? How could you let something like that happen? I thought you were a better person than that."

This wasn't going anywhere near as she'd hoped. "I am, Mike, I am better than that. It was a mistake."

"If you think before you do something you don't make mistakes like that."

"I called because I needed some understanding from you. We've always been close. Please don't be mad at me."

"No...sorry, Carla...this is something I *don't* understand. How could you do this to Keith?"

"Keith is okay."

"Really. Well, then that's one more thing I don't understand."

"It's me who's not okay."

"I don't know, I don't know...maybe you should go for some counseling instead of calling me."

"But, Mike…"

"Sorry. You've really lost me on this one, sis."

There was nothing more to be said between them. Mike took a stand against her behavior and that was that. When they hung up Carla felt more alone than ever. She would never have expected him, of all people, to let her down. She needed…needed…

She picked up the phone again and dialed Milo Printing.

"M-may I speak to Alonzo Quinn, please?" Carla asked, disguising her voice.

"Hi, Carla," Darcy recognized her.

"Please," Carla said.

It was surprising that Darcy didn't just hang up on her. But instead she took advantage of the opportunity to haggle her. "What goes around comes around, right?"

Carla waited.

With a cruel laugh, Darcy transferred her call to Alonzo.

"I need to see you again," Carla told him the instant he answered.

"What's wrong?" he asked as if he didn't know.

"Can you meet me for lunch somewhere again? Please, Alonzo?"

"No."

"But I—"

"This can't become a thing, you know."

"I know."

He sighed heavily. "Where are you?"

"Home."

"Alone?"

"Yes."

"See you there in a few minutes."

🍁   🍁   🍁

"This is ridiculous," Keith sputtered to Nathan as they met today's job.

"Yeah, I know," Nathan said. "But if Larson wants his garage painted purple, we paint it purple."

"No…I'm referring to me being the last one to find out."

"Carla? We're talking about Carla here?"

Keith nodded as he pried the cover off of his paint can.

"She told you last night," Nathan assumed, with a notable sound of relief.

Keith nodded again then headed for the north side of the garage with his supplies.

Nathan, taking nothing with him, paraded after him.

"I knew something was going on," Keith said, swiping his purple-loaded brush along the top wooden plank of the garage siding. "I had this gut feeling."

"You seem pretty calm about it."

"What else can I do?"

Nathan moaned. "You're a man, aren't you?"

"What the hell does that mean?"

"Carla deserves punishment."

"I'll ground her for a couple months, how's that?"

"Don't be glib, Keith. She cheated on you. Worse thing a wife can do. Don't be so easy on her."

"I love Carla. Yeah, it hurt me to hear what she'd done but I'm not going to break up with her because of it. She…she's hurting, too."

"Jeez…" Nathan said, shaking his head and starting to get his own supplies together. "If you don't come down hard enough on her, she just may do it again."

Keith stopped painting. He almost stopped breathing. "We're talking Carla here."

Nathan's warning continued. "We're talking about someone who cheated on you. How do you know for sure that it's not the beginning of new pattern rather than just a one-timer?"

"Because I…well, I suppose I don't know…but I trust her."

Nathan gave a crude laugh. "There's a worthless word. Alice and Carla…well, looks like they're two of a kind. Like mother, like daughter."

Keith stopped responding to his father-in-law's talk, and thus Nathan finally stopped talking. Nathan got seriously busy at his painting, and Keith was glad for the quiet.

As the morning crept along, Keith was finding that his job was not exactly the therapy he'd hoped it would be for his problems. He was feeling worse instead of better. He felt a little dizzy, enough that sometimes his vision blurred. It was a good thing he wasn't painting anything more intricate than a garage. Although his stomach wished the paint was any other color than purple. *Damn*, he felt lousy. Like he really didn't think he could hang in there a whole day. This had never happened to him before. But then Carla'd never cheated on him before.

Maybe he should go home. Maybe just seeing Carla there and being with her again would reassure him that they were still a couple, still okay. He needed reassurance. Nathan sure wasn't offering any.

❦   ❦   ❦

"You didn't have to come here," Carla told Alonzo as she led him into the living room. Though the way he was looking at her, she supposed her neediness was pretty evident. She motioned for him to take a chair then sat in the one across from him.

"You sounded terrible on the phone," he said. "You *look* terrible. So…how can I help you? Tell me what I can do."

"Be my friend," she said.

He smiled. "I am your friend, you know that. So we…you and I…we got a little out of line that night…but we can get past that."

"How?" Carla doubted.

"Time. Give it some time, Carla."

"I have!" she said. "So far, in the amount of time I've given it, I've lost my kids, my parents, probably my husband, and Darcy, and—"

"You haven't lost much with Darcy. Far as I'm concerned, she was a big nothing to begin with."

Carla was surprised to hear Alonzo say that. She'd always rated Darcy's popularity to be high with the guys at Milo.

Alonzo further stated, "We all saw through her long before you did. She shouldn't have blabbed to the others about what happened between you and me."

"I…I'm so alone now," Carla stated.

"You think you are, but no, Carla, you're not. Like I told you yesterday, you can come back to Milo. Everyone would welcome you in an instant. I think even Darcy would, because she's got more than she can handle at the desk now in your absence And…you've still got your husband, right? I mean, he wouldn't—"

"I don't know."

Alonzo's look was sympathetic and curious.

Carla sighed. "When I told Keith, he…he was upset but he took it better than I thought he would."

Alonzo shrugged. "That's good, right?"

"I don't think so. I mean, yeah, Keith's a quiet sort of guy, but he's giving me the impression that he doesn't really care what I did."

"No, I doubt he'd feel like that."

"You don't know him."

"No. But I know you, Carla, well enough to know what a lucky man Keith is to have you. Again…just give this whole thing some time."

Carla left her chair. "*Why*? Why did we have sex that night, Alonzo? What happened? Can you explain it to me? Because I still don't get it. I just don't."

He smiled compassionately. "From a woman's point of view no. But from mine probably yeah."

Carla scrinched her face, somehow knowing she wasn't going to like this.

"Lust," he said.

Still scrinching, she verified, "You didn't care for me? You only *lusted* for me?"

"I'm not an animal, Carla. Yes, of course I care for you. My lust came out of that."

If Alonzo thought that made it sound okay to her, well, it didn't. She'd almost, sort of, really begun thinking he was someone special, and that maybe *she'd* been someone special to him. But it was never more than a big mistake and she was a fool for having ever thought she could, in the slightest bit, analyze it into meaning anything more.

Alonzo came to put his arms around her. At first it sent a message to Carla that made her flinch away from him. But the look in his dark eyes soothed her and made it feel right when he again tried putting his arms around her. She allowed herself to rest her head against his shoulder. She was weary and his embrace felt good. She worked at trying to think of him as a friend rather than just a mistake. As she so needed a friend to lean on right now.

They talked for almost an hour. Alonzo didn't seem anxious to get back to work. It seemed his only concern of the moment was Carla. Beyond his manly lustfulness she believed he was a good person, a decent person. And she hoped beyond her womanly vulnerability she, too, was a good person.

When Alonzo decided to leave, Carla went to the front door with him. They said good-bye, and she thanked him for coming over. He stepped outside and she stayed in the opening.

After a moment's hesitation, he turned back and gave her a kiss. "Take care."

Carla watched him walk to his car in the driveway. Then she recognized the truck parked out along the street curb, partially hidden behind a Lilac bush. It was Keith's.

CHAPTER 17

Nathan was surprised when Keith returned to their paint job. From how his son-in-law looked when he'd left, Nathan hadn't expected him back. "You said you were sick and gonna go home."

"I was. I did." Keith resumed painting the section of garage he'd left but twenty minutes ago. There was a dark cloud hanging over him now.

Nathan stopped work to study him. "I don't get it."

"You don't want to," Keith assured him.

"Hell I don't!" Nathan responded. He stood watching Keith paint with the haphazardness of a six-year old and couldn't allow that. "Hey!" Nathan scowled. "You want me to fire you?"

"Yeah."

"Well, you're askin' for it, the way you're using that brush."

"Yeah," Keith agreed.

"Okay, you're fired!" Nathan said it like he meant it, but he didn't.

Keith threw his paint brush at a hedge of near-by bushes. Several leaves became the color purple. Then he sank down in the grass, saying, "He was there."

"Who? Where?"

"Carla's lover. I got home and there's this blue car in the driveway. So I parked in the street. Curiously. And just sat there. And pretty soon this guy comes out the front door, turns back and gives Carla a kiss. Then leaves. In the blue car."

"Whoa." Nathan suddenly understood Keith's misery. "What'd you do?"

"I came back here."

"That's it? You didn't—Carla didn't see you?"

- 119 -

"I don't think so."

"Why didn't you go in and confront her?"

"Because. Because I'm a nice guy and…and I'm giving her her space, y'know?"

"Shit, no! I *don't* know!"

Keith got back on his feet and went to retrieve his brush out of the bushes. "I love her. And I know she loves me. We…just have to get through this…this thing or whatever it is."

Nathan stood stunned at what'd happened and how Keith was reacting.

Keith cleaned his brush with a rag then began working on the garage again. "Just like you and Alice, right?" he compared.

"Right," Nathan said smugly, "which is why she's staying at the house and I'm staying with Ryan."

"I'm not talking physical space. It's about psychological space. Live together, just don't harp at each other. Marriage needs patience and space. At least…I guess it does."

"I'm from the old school," Nathan claimed. "Honesty and trust up front, forget the patience and space logic."

"Yeah…well…" Keith drawled, "maybe you're right."

"Yeah…" Nathan moaned, "well, maybe *you're* right. Jeez, I don't know."

🍁   🍁   🍁

Carla was sitting on the stoop out front of Ryan's apartment building late that afternoon when he came home from work. He had Jessie with him. The kids looked shocked, seeing her there, as if knowing this wasn't good.

"Mom," Ryan said on his approach.

She stood up, saying, "He knows. Your dad knows."

She didn't have to explain. Her children knew exactly what she was referring to.

The three of them went inside and up the stairs to Ryan's apartment. He offered to make some hot chocolate. Carla said no. Jessie said yes but went ignored.

Was there really anything more to say? Carla wondered nervously as she and Jessie sat down on the couch and Ryan, with his arms crossed, stood against a wall. Everyone stared at one another in awkward silence.

Finally Ryan asked, "Is Dad all right?"

"I don't know," Carla answered. "Actually, yeah, he might be more okay with this than I am."

"I don't get that," Jessie said. "I just don't get that at all."

"You're too young to get it," Ryan told her.

She gave a resentful huff.

"Jessie," Carla said, turning to her, "I want you to pack your things and come home with me."

Jessie's dark eyes sparked with defiance. "I live here now."

Carla was hurt by that, but Jessie was undoubtedly hurting even more. If Carla gave in, she'd at least make Jessie feel better, but easy wasn't always best. She had to be firm. She was, after all, the parent and Jessie was but thirteen. "Get your stuff together. *Now.*"

Jessie looked to her brother for a second opinion. He shook his head and shrugged, as if it were beyond him.

"*Tell her*, Ryan," Carla urged him, knowing the influence he had on his sister.

"Maybe you *should* go home," he advised Jessie.

"No!" Jessie protested. "I can't stand it there anymore after what's happened."

"We're still a family," Carla said. "I'm still your mother."

"This family's getting crazier and crazier," Jessie exclaimed.

Carla started to ask, "Grandpa told you about—"

"Yes," Jessie said.

Now Carla had to feel bad for that as well, making it all the harder for her to insist, "You're coming home."

"It's crazy here, too," Jessie argued, "but I choose to stay with Ryan."

Though it was clearly not easy for Ryan, he sided with his mother. "I think you should go, Jessie."

The girl was overwhelmed with disappointment. "You're a double-crosser, you know that, Ryan? You take me in and then you throw me out. I'm human, you know. I have feelings, you know."

Though he seemed sympathetic, he was nevertheless rejecting. "Jessie, you're a kid. Go with Mom."

Jessie stood from the couch. "Speaking of ages..." she looked at Carla as if she'd found something with which to save herself. "Ryan just happens to be dating a girl...actually a *woman*...way older than he. She's almost as old as you, Mom. They kissed. I saw them kiss. So what do you think of that? Maybe you should take *Ryan* home. Maybe he's too young and irresponsible to be on his own."

Carla and Ryan exchanged looks. This was just what Carla needed, something more to worry about. No, she didn't like the idea of her nineteen-year old son seeing an older woman. She couldn't believe he would do so. Except, yes, the sheepish look on his face acknowledged it was true.

"She's not that old," he offered. "She's thirty-two."

Carla wished she herself were only thirty-two. How could she be almost *forty*? She was too young to be forty. Keith had recently accused her of being in menopause. Forty was old. She didn't want to leave her thirties. She wasn't ready to start a whole new decade. But soon it would come and there was nothing she could do about it.

"Anyway," Ryan added. "she's not like my girlfriend or anything, she—"

"I guess your life is your life," Carla relented out of exhaustion.

"What about me?" Jessie balked. "I have a life too, you know."

Carla gave her a tender look.

"Everyone treats me like I don't," Jessie added.

What was the use? Carla thought. Force wasn't going to make this any easier for anyone. "Yes, you do have a life, a very precious one, Jessie. So I...I guess you can still stay here, if you want. For a while."

"Really?" Jessie was more shocked than relieved.

"*Thanks*," Ryan slurred sarcastically, more to himself than to Carla.

Carla gave him a smile, drawing a slight smile out of him. "I guess this will take some time," she said, having received that very advice from Alonzo earlier. "So let's give it that. Time. Just know that I love you both very much and I pray for your forgiveness."

As she started toward the door, Ryan caught her and gave her a hug. But Jessie stayed back, holding onto her hostility.

Carla went to her car, heavy-hearted and close to tears. She got in and headed for home, worrying what it was going to be like tonight with Keith. What had he been doing, parked before the house that morning when Alonzo had been there? What had he thought of it? Why didn't he come inside instead of just leaving again? She didn't know what it meant. She didn't know what anything meant anymore.

Carla was sitting in the swing when Keith came home from work. He came up the porch steps, asking playfully, "You're not cooking tonight?"

"TV dinners in the oven," she said.

"Oh."

"Okay?"

He laughed. "Damn, I suppose." He sat on the railing across from her, realizing she wasn't picking up on his humor. "You have a bad day today?"

"No. Why? You?"

"No. Why?'

They were chasing each other around the mulberry bush, waiting for the weasel to pop. Keith had seen Alonzo leaving the house that morning. Why wasn't he zeroing in on that? If he was waiting for her to mention it first, she wasn't going to.

Keith turned from Carla to glance across the back yard. "Ahh, spring…I'll be putting in my garden soon. And you'll be doing your flowers, right?"

When she didn't answer, he looked back and caught her quiet nod. She didn't understand his disinterest in what he'd seen earlier. It should have made him super curious. Super furious. His ignoring it bothered Carla more than if he'd gotten angry about it. She didn't understand.

"I'd better check on dinner," she said, leaving the swing.

"Hey…" Keith stopped her, only to ask, "so what *did* you do today?"

It was a hint for her to mention Alonzo's visit, but she wasn't going to. She simply told him, "I went to talk to the kids. I tried to get Jessie to come home, but she didn't want to. She's going to stay with Ryan for a while longer."

"And Nathan's staying there too, right?"

"Yes."

"I suppose the kids know about his not being your—"

"Yes," Carla said.

"Jessie will be okay there for a while," Keith made of it.

"And my dad, will he?"

"Sure, probably," Keith told her. "And so will we be okay, Carla."

He said it like he meant it. But how could he? she wondered. For some unknown reason that was scaring the heck out of her, he seemed to be taking this way too easily.

☙ ☙ ☙

"You shouldn't have mentioned my friend to Mom," Ryan scolded Jessie.

"Friend?" Jessie arched her eyebrows. "You mean your older-woman friend?"

"You know nothing about her. You know nothing about the adult world. You—"

"I'm learning pretty fast." Jessie stormed about her brother's small apartment, feeling both penned in and left out. Her head was crowded from all she had to endure these days. Nothing was making sense. Maybe everybody was right, telling her that she was just a kid. Maybe she just needed to go home to her own room and hug her teddy bear.

Amidst her self pity, a knock came at the apartment door. To Ryan's look of panic, Jessie rushed there ahead of him to open it.

It was his *older woman*.

Ryan shoved Jessie aside, stepped out into the hall and shut the door behind him.

Jessie paced the apartment, waiting for brother to come back in. It seemed like forever. When he did, she met him with a loaded look.

"Don't ask, okay?" he warned her.

"I deserve to know."

"How do you figure that?"

"I'm living with you, I'm a close part of your life, I have the right to know what's going on with you?"

Ryan stood in the middle of the living room, glaring at her. "You have no rights here! None!"

Jessie was next to crying. But she couldn't let go. She'd done too much of that lately. It was for sure one of the things that made her look like a kid. She had to be braver, older, tougher.

"Ryan—" she began.

"Yeah?" he answered apprehensively.

"We…we have this situation going on between Mom and Dad right now—"

"Yeah?"

"And Grandma and Grandpa."

"Yeah?"

"Meanwhile…we…we have our own lives, and—"

"I do, but I'm not so sure about you," he teased her.

"I…I just want you to know that I'm here for you…really…like if you want to talk to me about anything…any problems you might have or anything…okay?"

Looking totally amazed, he smiled and gave a nod.

CHAPTER 18

❦

"He knows and he doesn't care," Carla told her mother on the phone the next morning.

"Who? What?" Alice didn't get it.

Still in her robe and slippers, Carla stood in the kitchen with a mug of coffee in one hand, the phone in her other. "Keith. And you know what about."

"Oh, Carla, of course he cares. Why would you think he doesn't?"

"His actions. He acts like nothing happened. He's unfazed."

"Oh, Carla, I doubt that."

"If he cheated on *me* I'd hate him, I'd scream at him, I'd leave him."

"Mmm..." Alice sighed, "you're so like your father."

Carla paused before remorsefully confirming, "When you told Dad about Wayne, he left you."

"Well, there you go, dear. You criticize Keith's placid reaction, yet you don't like the opposite. Your Keith, he's being loving and understanding and he's still there. You've got to give him credit for that."

Carla gave it more thought. It sounded right, but it just didn't feel right. "I don't know. So far my honesty with him is making me feel worse than my lying to him did."

"I so wanted to protect you and Keith from having to deal with this."

"It was never your responsibility to do that."

Alice laughed softly. "Oh, Carla, a mother's responsibilities are unlimited."

"I'm not doing so well with Jessie. She hates me. She insists on staying with Ryan."

"She'll come around, dear. Give this some time. That's all you can do now."

Time. It seemed to be the key word in all of this. Yet so far time wasn't erasing Carla's problems as much as it seemed to be intensifying them. She wished she had *no* time, for thinking, worrying, contemplating. She had way too much time on her hands since leaving Milo. She needed to be busy. Crazy busy. Deeply involved in something other than herself.

After the phone call with her mother, which failed to enlighten Carla as she'd hoped, she dressed, poured some cleaning solution into a bucket of water and tackled the kitchen walls. They weren't noticeably dirty, but when she got done scrubbing them she hoped to feel noticeably better. Therapy in the rough.

Nathan stopped by unexpectedly at noon. He knocked once at the back door, saw through the screen door that Carla was standing on stepladder doing *something*, laughed, and let himself in. "What's going on?" he questioned.

"Hi." She looked down at him. "Washing walls."

The humor he'd walked in with was short-lived. His next question came off on a cantankerous snarl. "And that's a good thing for you to be doing at this particular time?"

Carla gave him a harder look. "What does that mean?"

"It means with the situation you're in you've got nothing better to do than wash your kitchen walls?"

Carla slammed her rag into the bucket of water, sending a splash through the air that nipped her father's shoulder. She came down from the ladder and faced him straightforwardly. "Have you got a better idea of what I should be doing? And if so, is it so amazing that you left your job to come tell me right now?"

"I'm on my lunch break. And I'm mad, yeah, I admit it."

"At me? Or Mom?"

"Right now the whole world."

"That's a lot of people."

"Well, to narrow it down for starters I'd love to get my hands around the neck of that guy you—"

"Leave Alonzo out of this!" Though Carla supposed she knew where this was headed, she was surprised by her defensive reaction.

"And just how do I do that?" Nathan fended.

"He…he's not solely to blame. I…he…it takes two to tango."

Nathan gave an unamused laugh. "I don't think this is about no damn tango."

Carla wiped her hands on the thighs of her jeans, then brushed her unruly hair back from her face, knowing she was as much of a mess on the outside as she was on the inside. "I made a mistake and I'm paying for it."

Nathan was about to say something, but Carla raised her hand for him to let her continue. "Mom made a mistake too, long ago, that she's been paying for all along. She tried to protect you from it. Can't you understand that? Appreciate that?"

Nathan shook his head. "Sorry, no."

"And you're so above that? You've never made a serious mistake in your life?"

"I've never cheated on Alice, no."

"There are other types of mistakes."

"None so bad."

"Lack of forgiveness might be one," she suggested.

"I'm an honest person, Carla, you know that. You've grown up with that. Alice, she lived with a lie between us all those years and that really stinks."

"Only because you found out about it," Carla reasoned. "And that was all because of what I did. She told you something painful in hopes of stopping you from telling Keith something painful. Of which I ended up telling him myself anyway. And you know what…? It's all one big freakin' joke because after all was said and done Keith doesn't really care."

Nathan's eyes narrowed. "What do you mean, Keith doesn't care?"

Carla gave a casual shrug. "I guess you could say that he's a man of today. Infidelity happens quite commonly in today's world, and Keith's an easy-going guy who just accepts that."

"That's a bunch of crap! Keith's easy-going, right, but he's not heartless and he's not stupid."

"Okay, let's put Keith and me aside and get back to you and Mom. You're throwing away forty-one years of good marriage because of one little problem that—"

"*Big problem.*"

"—happened years ago."

"It may have happened years ago," Nathan's voice reached the rise of hers, "but it's still right here staring me straight in the face."

"Fine!" Carla said. "If I bother you so much why don't you just go! You don't have to ever look at me, *your problem*, again!"

After a couple minutes her suggestion seemed to suit him and he left.

Carla was more upset than ever. Her father's harsh rejection hurt her in one way, while her husband's easy acceptance hurt her in another. The unfinished kitchen walls awaited her return. But she'd totally lost her energy.

Instead she opened a cupboard, took out a large bag of nacho chips, and went to the living room. She plopped into an easy chair, draped her legs over an arm of it, and started munching chips as an aide to soothe her soul. It sort of helped. There was a lot to be said for junk food.

🍁   🍁   🍁

"Spaghetti again?" Nathan complained, as he ate spaghetti at Ryan's kitchen-counter with his two grandchildren for the fourth night in a row.

"It's fine with me," Jessie said. She loved spaghetti. It was her favorite meal, next to pizza. She loved that Ryan stocked his cupboard with cans of it.

Ryan gave his grandfather a slanted look. "If the food doesn't suit you here, find a another place."

"I deserved that, didn't I?" Nathan admitted. "Suppose a kid like you can't be making that gooda money yet, right?"

"We mechanics do okay," Ryan said.

"I think he spends it all on his girlfriend," Jessie offered. "Whoops... *woman friend.*"

"Well, now..." Nathan's interest broadened.

"He's dating an older woman," Jessie explained.

"Stop it!" Ryan warned her. "You don't know anything about my personal life." He left the counter, taking a slice of bread with him to eat as he wandered about the apartment.

"I'd say your reaction is most revealing," Nathan concluded.

Jessie laughed. "Yeah, *look* at him."

"And how about you two?" Ryan asked. "Your reaction to family problems. Instead of facing them where they need facing, you come running to me."

Nathan and Jessie exchanged looks, shrugged, nodded agreeably, turned quiet, and continued eating.

"Look," Ryan said, firmly but tenderly, "I took you guys in because I care, but I can't keep you here forever."

"Is this an eviction notice?" Nathan asked, taking a second helping of spaghetti out of the serving bowl, despite his criticizing it.

Jessie's giggle was brief. Then she scowled at Ryan, "It's amazing that you seem to be giving more consideration to that *woman* than to your own family."

Ryan said nothing.

As though Nathan felt sorry for him, he told him, "We each have our own ways in dealing with things. Y'know what…this spaghetti ain't too bad, Ryan."

Jessie pushed her brother further. "Just because you have this apartment, you think you're disconnected from us?"

A helpless smile slid over his face. "Yeah, I'd hoped I was."

"Grandpa and I…we've shared our feelings with you. So why don't you share your feelings about your lawyer girlfriend with us?"

"I told you, Grace is not a lawyer. And she's not my girlfriend."

"Ah-ha…" Nathan said, "she has a name."

"Well, maybe you're not dating her," Jessie carried on, "but you sure were kissing her outside your door the other day."

Nathan put his fork down, wiped his mouth with a paper napkin, and commented with a grin, "Isn't this an interesting diversion from Carla and Alice. Come on, Ryan…tell us more about Grace."

Looking cornered in his own apartment, Ryan began to weaken under pressure. "You guys are too much, you know that?"

"We are," Nathan admitted, "only because we love you."

"We do," Jessie enforced it. "So let's talk."

"Okay," Ryan said, retaking his stool at the counter. "This older woman," he began in the manner of a hefty confession, "she's not my girlfriend. Not in the way you guys are thinking. I mean, yeah…she's my friend. And uh…she's come over to talk with me a few times. She…she's got problems, see, and…and she's needed some comforting. And…and she lives right down the hall…with…with her husband."

"*You're seeing a married woman?*" Jessie exclaimed, finding this far worse than she'd expected.

"Jeez!" Nathan's reaction was the same.

"You're no better than Mom," Jessie laid judgement on him.

Ryan nodded solemnly. "I uh…I was beginning to see that myself, you know? I mean, like Grace sort of blinded me on the reality side at first. But, uh, yeah…Mom's situation made me look at stuff in a different way. And so I…uh, yesterday I told Grace to take her problems elsewhere because I didn't want to get involved like that. I encouraged her to work on her marriage problems with her husband, not somebody else. Such as me."

Jessie gave her brother a slow, satisfied smile.

And Nathan raved, "Good boy."

Ryan gave way to a smile of his own, backed with notable relief.

"I'm sorry I pushed," Jessie apologized.

Ryan nodded. "You're a very pushy little sister, that's for sure."

"Sounds to me," Nathan said, "like you've done some growing up, Ryan. I'm proud of you."

In turn Ryan asked him, "So when are *you* going to grow up, Grandpa?"

Nathan pretended to take offense. "I'd grow up a lot faster if you started serving steak around here instead of spaghetti."

"Shall I get out the tinker toys?" Ryan suggested.

"You have some? *You actually have some*?" Nathan was genuinely excited.

"I do," Ryan said. "Brought 'em with me when I left home. You and Grandma gave them to me when I was seven."

Nathan left the counter with childlike eagerness, and Ryan laughed on his way to fetch them.

"I'll do dishes," Jessie offered.

CHAPTER 19

Carla knew she shouldn't have done it, asked Alonzo to meet her again. But a day came when she felt especially down and desperate and weakened. Thus she called him at work and they met in the park for lunch.

"I'm sorry. This wasn't a good idea," she said, unwrapping her Subway sandwich.

"You said you liked Subways when I asked you, so that's what I brought." He was grinning, knowing perfectly well what she meant but razzing her.

"No, I mean our getting together again."

"Your idea."

"I know."

The way they smiled at each other lent acceptance over fault.

Carla started to eat her sandwich. It tasted good, better than anything she'd ate at home lately. She gazed at the trees and the overall beauty of Tag Lake Park. A strange but recognizable sense of peacefulness came over her for being with Alonzo that she hadn't been able to find with anyone else these days. It was strange how he was both the cause and the cure to her problem.

He caught her studying him and offered, "I know how much agony that night's still causing you and I wish I knew how to make it better for you."

"Your being here, meeting me like this, helps."

His response was but a nod, as he'd just taken a bite out of his sandwich.

"It's strange about that night, isn't it," she said. "How it happened. How one thing lead to another and another."

"That's usually the way it begins."

"I'm seriously trying to sort this out," Carla said.

"But you can't. What happened, happened. Let it go and get on with your life."

"You make it sound so easy."

"I don't mean to. Life is hard. You can't always explain everything, you just have to go along."

"I've lost my family."

"I think it's more that you've lost yourself, Carla. Your family…I'm sure they love you and haven't give up on you."

"*Keith's* given up on me."

"What do you mean?"

"When I finally told him what happened, he took it well and—"

"That's good. Isn't it?"

"It means he doesn't care."

"I don't believe that."

"It's true. He doesn't have a jealous bone in his body, I found that out. He's more like…oh, well, no problem…I forgive you, dear, and we'll just pretend it never happened."

"He said those things?"

"Implied them."

Alonzo laughed and took another bite of his sandwich. "And I suppose in that silly little mind of yours that only means—"

"He doesn't care," Carla insisted. She rewrapped her sandwich, set it on the bench, and stood up. "It doesn't matter to Keith what I do. I mean, if he loved me it would matter, right? Well, it…it just doesn't matter."

Alonzo was quiet for a few minutes. Then he grinned and suggested, "We could try harder to *make* him jealous."

It wasn't funny to Carla. Alonzo was quick to get that and rose to give her an apologetic hug. "He's a fool, that husband of yours."

Carla felt all too comfortable in his embrace. *Damn him. Damn the situation.* She allowed herself to nestle her head against his shoulder and close her eyes. Why did he have such a calming effect on her? She was supposed to get that from Keith. She *wanted* to get that from Keith. But since that Friday night…

"Carla," Alonzo broke her thoughts, "I'd take back that night if I could."

She stepped away from him, surprised.

He questioned her reaction, "You didn't want to hear that?"

She smiled uneasily. "Yes and no."

He smiled back. "You can't have two answers. Only one."

"Then I'll make it an I don't know."

"Don't you? Know?"

She shook her head with another, "I don't know. Keith saw us together the other day. When you were leaving my house."

"He was there? Where?" Getting caught seemed to alarm Alonzo more than anything did thus far about the situation.

"For some unknown reason he came home from work right at that time, parked along the curb, and saw us."

"Oh, I'm sorry, Carla. That must have really flamed the fire."

She shook her head. "He drove away. And later he never said a word about it."

"You're kidding."

Carla shrugged it off matter-of-factly. "I *told* you, he doesn't care. He has his life, and he doesn't much care what I do with mine."

"And…" Alonzo said with an off-sided look that seemed half teasing and half serious, "so what *do* you want to do with it, your life?"

"I don't know."

"Come back to Milo," he suggested.

"No."

"John hasn't hired a replacement yet. I could talk to him and—"

"Never."

Alonzo sighed heavily. "Okay. How about I talk to Keith?"

"No!" Carla said, clearly inferring that was the last thing she wanted.

"I don't know what else to say or do to help you."

She gave him a sad smile. "Hey, a Subway and a hug work wonders."

"Well then, what do you say we sit back down and finish our sandwiches, and then after one more hug I get back to my job."

"Bet you didn't know," Carla said before sitting, "that my Dad painted this bench."

Alonzo observed the setting in a whole new way.

"All of them in the park," she added. "He and Keith."

Alonzo nodded and took a bite of his sandwich.

The silence between Carla and Keith, as they sat in the living room after supper that night, was as discomforting as a deafening noise. Keith was reading his book, or at least *pretending* to read, and Carla was staring at the cover of a magazine.

It was Keith who finally spoke first. "Find a job yet?"

It was the like the last straw to Carla's overloaded day, causing her to burst out of her chair in a release of what she'd been trying all along to hold back. "With everything that's been going on lately, you're most concerned whether or not I have another job?"

Keith put his book aside. "It seemed important to you, getting a job, yeah. I'm interested in what's important to you, Carly. Don't have a bird."

One more last straw. "I'll have a bird if I want to! And I'll get another job when I get another job!"

When Keith covered his ears, she raised her voice even more. "You…you act so cool and so quiet and…and then you—"

"I was simply trying to open a conversation," he said.

"Good subject."

"Got another one?"

"I don't know. *Do I?* There could be one that might interest you more than whether or not I found a job."

"Name it," he said smugly.

"Like I have to?"

Keith popped out of his chair and came toward her. "Where the hell are you coming from, Carla?"

"I guess maybe from the obvious fact that my husband *doesn't* know where I'm coming from."

He shrugged, shook his head, and turned out his hands.

"There," she said, taking that as proof.

He said nothing. He still didn't get it.

"It…it's very rejecting to me," she tried to explain.

"Rejecting…" he turned the word back on her. "Aren't you the one who did the rejecting?"

A few minutes ago Carla had longed for an ice-breaking talk between them. Now that it'd started she felt the need to drop it before it went too far. She started to leave the room, but Keith grabbed her roughly by the arm and kept her.

"You're the one, Carla, who was unfaithful," he reminded her. "So exactly what is it, in regards to that, that you want from me?"

She stood cinched in his grasp, hating that their talking more was worse than their non-talking. Hating his temper over his clemency. Confused by the switch. She gave him a long look ahead of saying, "Yes, I was unfaithful. Which turned out being kind of a test."

"Test?" he questioned.

"You failed it."

Keith was about to say something, but Carla burst ahead of him with, "It proved that you're really not interested enough in me for it to matter one way or the other to you what I did."

Keith frowned. "Hasn't it sort of looked more like *you're* the one who's not interested enough?"

Carla hated that he was right. She hated that she didn't know where to go with this now that she'd driven him from passive to aggressive. "I…it…had nothing to do with you."

Keith released his hold of her in the line of giving her a little shove. "Like I was just a nobody in the picture?"

They were into it now, and Carla had to go all the way to get her needed answers. "You were somebody, of course, but—"

"Not that night, I wasn't. Look, Carla, I've been trying to forget and forgive, but you're not especially making that easy for me."

"Is that what you've been doing? Forgetting and forgiving?"

"*Hello*…I'm still here. I haven't packed my bag and left. Doesn't that tell you something?"

"Why?" was all she could ask.

"Why what?"

"Why don't love me enough to—"

"*To what*?" Keith threw up his hands.

"—show me?"

Keith looked totally lost in the discussion. "If you think I haven't showed you, you must be totally blind."

"You…you haven't expressed the normal male feelings I would have expected."

"Huh?"

"Nothing," she backed down.

"Normal male feelings?"

"Nothing," she said again.

Keith grabbed her again, tight enough this time that it really hurt. "Define normal male feelings…that I'm evidently lacking."

Tears were stinging in Carla's eyes. Not because her arm hurt or her feelings hurt, but because she feared she'd pushed a bad situation to worse.

"Christ, Carla!" Keith shouted in her face. "Don't you know that I've been going through hell over what you did? You think that because I've been mild-mannered about it that I've lost interest in caring about you, and about what you do, and about our marriage? I've been trying to be good to you. I've been assuming, although I may have been wrong, that you've been suffering as much or more than I have over this. I've been trying to give you what I thought you needed right now, Carly…my love and my help to get through this. Didn't you get that?"

She looked at him with more confusion than ever. "If you loved me," she said shakily, "you'd be so pissed off that you—"

Keith laughed amidst her words. "I've never laid a hand on you, if that's what you're talking about! And I don't intend to start now. Unless…of course…you really want that from me."

"That's not what I want!" she screamed.

"Well, what?" he demanded. "Tell me what the hell that is! Because I'm not understanding this conversation at all."

"I…I would have expected you to—"

"Yeah?" he prompted her. Then spoke ahead of her with, "You're running me in circles here, you know?"

"I thought if you just got mad, really mad, instead of really quiet and nice, I'd—"

"Okay! I'm mad! I'm damn mad! I've been damn mad since you first told me about you and him! On top of that, I saw him leaving the house the other day and giving you a kiss!"

"It wasn't what it appeared, you don't understand."

"I certainly wish I did." Keith picked up the footstool and threw it against the wall. The wall cracked in three directions.

Carla stared at the damaged wall. It was supposed to be a good sign. A sign that showed how truly upset he was because he truly loved her. Instead it scared her. "I don't like you like this."

"Oh, yeah? Well, you've got it now! The quote *normal* unquote man who shows his love in violence not empathy. I'm more normal than you thought, Carla. I'm just an average, normal guy who never expected his wife to cheat on him and when she did didn't know what the hell to do about it.

Carla was scared of where this was going. And Keith turned away from her as if he himself was also scared of where this might go.

"I…I'm sorry," she said to his back.

"For what? For your mistake or mine?"

She didn't give him an answer. There *was* no answer.

Keith stormed out of the room and headed upstairs. After a few minutes Carla went up to check. When she entered the bedroom, he was stuffing some clothes into a duffel bag.

"What are you doing?" she asked.

He sent her a self-explanatory look.

"Okay, okay…" Carla cried. "I didn't want you to be mad either. That's not what I wanted. Keith, don't leave. You don't have to leave. I'm sorry for everything. Most of all for doubting your feelings. Please…don't go away…I need you."

He paused for a moment. Though not with reconsideration. In the next moment he was taking his bag with him, leaving the room and thundering down the stairs.

Carla's whole body was shaking in the wreckage of her mistake. Not the mistake she made with Alonzo, but the one she made by misjudging Keith. She heard his truck start in the driveway, and it cut her like a double-edged knife. But surprisingly soon the hurt subsided and she only felt numb. Surely she was dead.

CHAPTER 20

❀

When Carla finally felt brave enough to go downstairs, she found the house hauntingly silent. As if there'd been a death. Yes, surely it had been hers. Keith had left and her life had ended right there. And she deserved it.

She would go sit in the porch swing for a while. And cry. And feel sorry. And regret that she hadn't known Keith like she should've known Keith. She'd misjudged his character badly. And that seemed to hurt him more than her cheating on him had. She was almost forty. She was supposed to be getting better and wiser at life by now, not worse. She'd messed up her whole family because of…

As Carla stepped out onto the dark porch, she was startled at finding Keith in the swing. "I thought you left," she said.

"No." His voice was barely a whisper.

"I heard your truck."

"I was that close to leaving, but I didn't."

Carla stood in place, afraid to move, afraid to say anything more, afraid to think what Keith might be thinking.

He motioned her over to the swing. "C'mere…let's talk."

She took a deep breath and went to sit beside him. "I think we both said quite a bit already."

"I've calmed down."

Carla wondered if that was a good sign or a bad sign. If only she and he could go back to before that Friday night. She knew that no one got through life without problems, but why did theirs have to be one of infidelity? She and Keith could have sailed through any other problem in the world besides this one. Their love had been so sweet and strong from the very start. How could something this stupid have happened to them?

"I wouldn't blame you if you'd want a divorce," she said. She could see, despite the darkness, that Keith had been crying. Something she'd only ever seen him do once before in their life together, and that had been at his brother's funeral three years ago.

"Carla," be began slowly, "what you did ripped me apart. I haven't dealt with this as easily as you'd thought. But I knew that leaving this marriage would rip me apart even more so I tried…I tried to—"

"Unhappy marriages aren't worth saving," Carla stated.

"Is that what *you've* been, unhappy?"

"No. I meant you."

"I'm not unhappy," Keith said. "I'm sad. And I'd really like to know where you're at, Carla, with all of this now. And…and where you were at *before* this."

She hung her head. "That's exactly what I've been grueling over myself. Because I don't know why I did what I did. And…and there's an even worse part to it."

Keith waited for her to go on.

"That night," she continued, "I was upset over missing Jessie's play. At Milo's party it was really bringing me down. Everyone was drinking and having a good time, and eventually I decided that maybe I should try something in hopes that it might give me a lift. So I let Marty mix me a drink. He called it his specialty, just for me. And it tasted good and I—"

"—had so many of them you helplessly fell into a little to-do with your fellow co-worker," Keith curtly finished her sentence.

"No, not exactly." Carla wrung her hands on her lap. "This is so hard."

"Well, I'm glad it's not easy for you," he said.

"I…I found out, since that night, that the drinks Marty made for me were non-alcoholic."

Keith was silently surprised.

"I'm not a drinker," Carla continued, "so how was I to know there was nothing in mine? The drinks, they just tasted so good that I figured they totally hid the taste of liquor. But come to find out, several days later, they'd contained no liquor at all."

"And…so…you were totally sober when you—"

"Yes."

"Totally responsible for your actions."

"Because of the mood I was in, along with drinking several drinks that I *believed* were alcoholic, well I guess it gave me the effect of being under the influence."

Keith looked dubious and she didn't blame him.

"Really," she said, "I've since heard that if you believe you're becoming inebriated then your system might actually respond that way."

"You *wanted* to feel that way?"

"No. I mean, yes. I was sort of trying to escape my downer but—"

"Into the arms of your co-worker?"

"No. It wasn't like that." Carla left the swing and walked across the porch to the railing. She turned there and looked back at Keith. "I was trying to relax."

"With your co-worker."

"No. I thought I was drinking booze, and I thought I was feeling lifted by that or…or something. And then when Alonzo—"

"Alonzo," Keith said the name resentfully.

"Alonzo was very nice to me and I was sort of feeling different, out of myself, you know, thinking that I was under the influence of those drinks. And it…all together…well, it…it sort of gave me permission."

"Permission?" Keith asked hesitantly.

"Subconsciously," she explained.

"Oh," Keith said. "Like you weren't operating under the influence of alcohol but rather under the influence of your subconscious."

Carla returned to sit with him in the swing. She put her hand on his knee and looked closely at him.

His face, in the dark, implied he wasn't getting this at all the way she'd hoped he would. And now his immediate rise out of the swing and away from her implied he didn't want to hear anymore. He went inside the house and Carla was again left alone, feeling ever so much worse for having tried to talk to Keith about this than if she hadn't tried at all. And for criticizing his quietness only to find his harshness far worse.

🍁   🍁   🍁

Though Keith didn't feel it, he acted as pleasant the next morning as if last night had never happened. Carla acted the same. She'd gotten up before him and had coffee and scrambled eggs ready when he came downstairs. They smiled at one another and chatted about things such as the news, the weather, and which video to rent next. But behind their niceties Keith was feeling the tension of a troubled marriage.

They kissed goodbye before he went out the door. God, he loved Carla so much, but it felt so different now. There were threats mixed into it now. It wasn't as comfortable as it'd once been. What could he do? He couldn't just snap his fingers and make it better. Maybe all he could do was give it some time.

Time. Yes. And in a manner of time Keith joined Nathan on their job twenty minutes late.

Nathan wisecracked, "How about I get you a new alarm clock for your birthday."

Keith moaned. "I had a rough night, okay?"

"Yeah, had a few myself lately. Your son's got a lumpy mattress."

"Anyway…it's not *my* birthday coming up, it's Carla's."

"Yeah, I know."

"The big 4-O," Keith stressed.

"For forty years I thought she was my daughter."

"She *is* your daughter, Nathan. Come on, quit doing this to her and to Alice and to yourself. Move back home and quit moochin' off Ryan."

Nathan laughed. "Did you know he pretty much lives on spaghetti?"

"Alice is a great cook. Go home, Nathan."

"Yeah…maybe…we'll see."

The guys worked side by side quiet for a while. Quiet of words, though the screeching noise of scraping loose paint off the house was excruciating.

"Carla and I talked last night," Keith eventually told his father-in-law. "I mean, really talked."

"And?"

"There's a lot of junk sitting in our marriage right now."

"*Tell* me about it."

Keith sighed and gave a nod. "Alice cheated on you, Carla cheated on me."

"Yeah, who would've thought?"

Keith swept a section of the wood siding with a wire brush.

Nathan stopped working to stare up at the dismal sky. "Whatdya say we shuck the painting for today and go have a few drinks?"

Keith looked at him. "I've never known you to shuck your work. Or for that matter to have a few drinks in the day time."

"It's going to be raining in another hour or so and we don't have any inside work scheduled. Come on."

"What are you saying?'

"The weather. And plan B." He motioned to the sky, pleading, "Come on, *rain*! I am so in the mood for plan B."

Keith grinned and took a guess, "Booze."

Thunder rumbled in the distance like an answer from higher up.

🍁   🍁   🍁

Carla sat nervously in the waiting room. If low lighting, plump chairs and soft music were supposed to relax her, they didn't. She was more scared now than when she'd called earlier to make an appointment. She'd never been to a psychologist before and wasn't sure she wanted to be now. But somehow she'd gotten herself there and had committed herself to trying it.

Her ten-minute wait before being called in seemed like an hour. And then the thirty minutes it took for her to tell the gypsy-dressed woman therapist the whole story of her mistake seemed like several hours. Carla only wanted this to be over quickly and favorably, instant relief, but so far it was tedious and humiliating.

"And you came here hoping to learn why you were unfaithful to the husband you love," the therapist surmised in a quiet, collected manner when Carla finally stopped pouring her heart out.

"Yes," Carla responded wearily.

"Keith…he came into your life when you were pretty young, didn't he?"

"Yes," Carla said.

"And you didn't know many boys before Keith who—"

"Well…a few, yes, but—"

"*Sexually*," the therapist clarified, looking at Carla over the top of her glasses.

This woman didn't beat around the bush. Though Carla was somewhat taken aback by her bluntness, she trusted her lead. "Keith, he was the first one, the only one, who I did it with."

"Had sex with."

Carla nodded.

The woman smiled. "It's okay to say the word sex." Then moving along, she asked, "Did you ever, in your marriage, feel a little cheated or—"

"I never cheated on Keith before now."

"No, no, dear…I mean did you ever, *you*, over the years, feel cheated that you never…well, that you never really experimented…had sex…with anyone else before Keith?"

"No," Carla answered quickly. Too quickly perhaps. Because with some delayed thought, she leaned forth, wondering, "Are you suggesting that subconsciously I was longing to see what it would be like to be with another man? Even though I was perfectly happy with Keith?"

The therapist fingered her multiple strands of beads and raised her eyebrows. "I'm not suggesting, I'm asking."

"My answer is no," Carla said resentfully.

The therapist's silence gave Carla the impression that her answer might be wrong. Thus she reconsidered. "I…I don't *think* I was having those thoughts.".

"The subconscious is amazing."

"I thought I was a stronger person than that, to…to be led by my subconscious. If…if I was."

The therapist checked her notes. "You were weakened by the guilt of having to miss your daughter's school play. None of us really know what we might be capable of when we're weakened. You were sad and vulnerable that night, and Alonzo…well, he sort of came into the picture like the soothing fix you needed right then and there."

"That's sick!" Carla responded.

"I'm trying to help you dig deep for a reason here."

"There is none. I honestly believe there is none."

"Maybe not one you care to admit, but there is one, Carla. There has to be."

Carla shook her head against it.

The therapist continued digging, "You liked it, didn't you?"

"What?" Carla asked. "Liked *what*?"

"Being with Alonzo that night."

Ouch. That was pretty deep. Carla didn't like going that deep. She'd come to the psychologist in hopes of feeling better, not worse.

"It's easier dealing with a problem if you first really get to the core of it," the therapist pointed out.

"And liking what I did with Alonzo is the core?"

"Could be. Subconsciously. Given your inexperience with men before Keith."

Carla held her head. "God, I'm worse than I thought I was."

"Carla, Carla…" the therapist spoke gently, "what you did wasn't right, by any means, any reason. It's just that if you understand what's truly behind it you can better deal with it, let it go, get beyond it."

"What about Keith? What do I do about Keith?"

"I can tell how much you love your husband. You didn't turn to Alonzo because you were unhappy with Keith. It was a combination of many things working on you that night, plus the curiosity of what it might be like with another—"

"I'm not liking this," Carla protested, getting up from her chair.

"You don't have to like it, dear. You only have to see it in order to let go of it."

Carla looked at the wall clock.

The therapist said, "Sit down. We've got twenty minutes left. And a lot more to uncover. And…I see this as going well, Carla. I really do."

Carla retook her seat, giving way to a slight smile.

Keith didn't come home for supper that night. Nor did he call. Nor did Carla have any idea where he could be. She kept the meal warm as long as possible, then she ate hers and put Keith's in the fridge.

Maybe he'd left her for real now. Now that she finally felt like she was getting her head straightened out. But when she went upstairs to check, she found his duffel bag still in the closet and none of his clothes seemed to be missing.

As she was going back down the stairs, the phone rang and she rushed to get it in the kitchen.

"Hi, Mom." It was Ryan.

In that very instant Carla pictured Keith lying in a hospital bed in critical condition. "What happened? Tell me what happened? I've been so worried and—"

"Slow down. Dad's okay. He's here at my place."

Carla let out a sigh of relief before asking again, "What happened?"

"On my way home from work I happened to see Grandpa's and Dad's trucks in the lot next to Barry's Bar. Something made me feel like I should stop and check things out."

Carla leaned against a cupboard counter for support. "And they were—"

"Yeah. They'd been there pretty much all day. They weren't real smashed, but sort of smashed. I took their truck keys and…and I insisted they come home with me."

"That was good, Ryan," Carla decided, if anything at all could be good right now.

"Barry approved of their trucks being left in his lot overnight. And I brought Dad and Grandpa here."

When Carla didn't say anything, Ryan asked, "Are *you* okay?"

"Let me talk to your father."

"He's asleep on the bed already. With Grandpa. It's okay, Mom. They're safe. I'm handling it. I…I kind of think Dad had this night coming to him. Know what I mean?"

Carla knew. And tried to accept it as Keith's needed outlet. But right now she desperately needed one of her own.

After hanging up from Ryan she took the phone again, thinking of Alonzo. Then she called herself *stupid* and instead went out on the porch to sit in her swing.

CHAPTER 21

Carla was glad when morning came. She'd barely slept last night and daylight came as a blessing. She was still lying in bed, absorbed in the beautiful burst of sunshine coming through the windows, when the phone rang. She grabbed it off the nightstand.

"It's me," Keith said.

"Hi, *me*," she said, with a smile in her voice and a knot in her stomach.

"Carly, I'm sorry about last night. Ryan said he called to let you know."

"It must be getting pretty crowded at his apartment."

Keith laughed. "It is. Kid's got a big heart."

"Too bad he doesn't have a bigger apartment."

Keith laughed again. "Yeah."

"I went to see a psychologist yesterday," she thought she should tell him.

"Oh…?" Keith was notably surprised.

"She…she was sort of reassuring, I guess."

"We're going to be all right, Carla. I could've told you that. I think I already *did* tell you that."

She shifted her position against the pillows, saying nothing.

"Sorry about last night," Keith apologized again. "Your dad came up with the idea and I was easily talked into it. It started raining. By noon we were out of work. We went to Barry's. Bet we played twenty games of pool."

"It's okay," Carla told him.

"Anyway…Ryan's about to give your dad and me a ride to our trucks, and then we'll go right to work. Unless you want me to come home first or—"

"No. Go. If your hangover's not too bad."

"I'll make it. Heck, if your dad can make it, so can I. To be sure…we'll be painting very quietly today. You okay, Carla?"

Since she still hadn't experienced what a true hangover felt like, she thought it couldn't feel much worse than having gone all night without sleep. "I'm okay," she told him.

"See you tonight," Keith said.

"Tonight," she agreed.

Carla hung up the phone, pulled herself out of bed, and headed for the shower. Then she would get dressed and go downstairs and have coffee on the porch swing. She would have a lot of thinking to do today. As if she hadn't already spent her whole long, sleepless night mulling things over in her head.

The therapist made Carla say a lot of things yesterday that she hated saying, but strangely enough she was relieved by it. And then they'd set up another appointment for next week, which Carla also had mixed feelings about. She felt as if she were being sentenced to a lifetime of therapy because of her mistake. But therapy was her own idea, not anyone else's. And she supposed the battle was half-won at that.

Nathan came by unexpectedly at noon, finding Carla, by then, sitting at the kitchen table with the newspaper and a red pen. "About last night," he began. "It was my fault. Keith didn't want to drink. I made him. Blame me."

"You came all the way here to tell me that?" she asked, more surprised than appreciative.

He sat down on another chair. "Keith and me…well, we did a lot of talking yesterday. And it was good. I'm gonna make up with your mom. She did me wrong a long time ago, but there's been a lot of good years between us that shouldn't get thrown away because of one mistake."

"*Me*," Carla took it to mean.

Nathan laughed, "Yeah…guess you did come along by way of a mistake, but what a wonderful, precious mistake to behold. You're a gift, Carla, that any man would be proud to call his daughter. And I *do* call you my daughter."

Carla was emotionally rocked and close to crying, but she blinked hard instead. "And you've forgiven Mom?"

"Yeah, what the hell…I'm still hopelessly in love with her."

Carla laughed. "I like hearing you say that."

"Yeah," he agreed, "me too. So what about you and Keith? Guess he phoned you from Ryan's this morning."

Carla answered, "We still love each other."

"Of course you do. Nothing will ever change that, Carla. *Nothing.*"

"I know," she had to say.

Nathan picked up the newspaper from the table. "Job hunting?"

Half joking, half serious, she said, "How does, *welcome to McDonald's, may I take your order* sound?"

"You gotta be kidding."

She shook her head. "That's about all that's out there."

"I think you can do better than that."

"I don't think so."

"Maybe I can help."

She shrugged. "I doubt it, but thanks."

He got to his feet, saying, "I better get back. Keith should be back from his errand, too, by now."

"What kind of an errand did he have?" Carla asked.

"Uh…he said he had some business at Milo Printing."

🍁   🍁   🍁

"Well, well…" Darcy greeted Keith's entrance at Milo Printing. Her dark eyes danced over him like a child's over a new toy. "And what may I help you with today?"

"You can direct me to Alonzo," Keith said straightforwardly.

His somberness hardened Darcy's expression. "You come to challenge him to a duel?"

"I came to talk to him, Darcy, not you. Would you please get him?"

"May I ask why?"

"No, you may not."

"I need to—"

"It's none of your business."

"Ah, but it *is* my business. I run this desk and everything in this company goes through me."

"Do you want to get him for me," Keith raised his voice, "or shall I search him out myself?"

Darcy stared at Keith as if she were trying to figure out his visit. But she couldn't. Finally she lifted her phone, pressed a button, and told Alonzo someone wanted to see him out front.

Keith waited nervously. Of *course* he was nervous, meeting the guy his wife cheated on him with. Darcy looked nervous, too, as if she expected a fight to break out the minute Alonzo appeared. But there was not going to be a fight. It was not Keith's intention.

A tall, handsome, slightly scruffy-looking guy came from a side door. He looked at Keith, as anyone would give a first look at a supposed customer, and asked, "May I help you?"

Not feeling free, with Darcy standing there gaping, Keith motioned to the front door, asking the print-shop guy, "Mind stepping outside with me, please?"

Alonzo gave him a questioning look, but nevertheless went.

"I'm Keith Wade," Keith introduced himself the minute they got outside.

"Ahh…" Alonzo said, "so that's what this is about."

Whatever Alonzo was probably suspecting, Keith bitterly resented it. "You don't *know* what this is about, so why don't you just shut up and let me tell you."

No doubt over-run with guilt, Alonzo started to apologize. "Look, I'm sorry about what happened between Carla and me. It shouldn't have happened and I—"

"I don't want to hear you explain your having had sex with my wife," Keith said. "I'm here to place a print job order."

Alonzo stood stunned and speechless.

"You do print jobs here, right?" Keith verified.

"W-what kind of print job are you talking about?"

Keith gave a smart laugh. "Print…words on paper."

"Oh. That kind."

"And free of charge, by the way." Keith took a piece of paper out of his pocket and unfolded it before Alonzo.

Nathan had said that he, too, had an errand to take care of on his lunch time, but he was already back painting when Keith returned to their site. His father-in-law tried his hardest to wrangle his reason for going to Milo Printing out of him, but Keith refused to talk about it.

After work, and before heading home, Keith went to Ryan's apartment to talk to his kids. Ryan was in the kitchen preparing supper and Jessie was on the couch doing homework. Keith grinned at the picture, having never seen such peacefulness between the two of them when they'd both lived at home. Maybe he just missed them in the worst way.

"Suppose you're wondering why I'm here," he began.

"If you're looking for a place to stay, I suppose it's okay," Ryan offered. "Grandpa moved back with Grandma."

"I haven't left home and I don't intend to. Your mom and I…we're okay. And we're going to work at being even more than okay."

"You've forgiven her? Just like that?" Jessie balked.

"Not *just like that*," Keith said. "It's a problem that'll take lots of work to get through, but I think your mom and I are capable of that."

"I don't get it," Jessie said.

"You're too young," Ryan razzed her.

"Speaking of which," Keith said to her, "you're coming back home. You're thirteen, Jessie, and you belong at home."

"But why can't—"

"Because I'm your father and I say so."

"And…and you and Mom are really going to be okay?"

"Yes. I promise."

Jessie gave her brother a look, then slowly shifted it back to Keith. A girlish smile melted over her cute face. How Keith had missed that sparkle in his daughter.

"Okay," she told him.

"Sunday," he gave her the precise moving day. "Which is your mom's birthday. I'll get a cake and let's celebrate it with her about two o'clock, okay? What do you say?"

"Sounds good to me," Ryan said.

"Thirty-nine?" Jessie questioned her mother's age to be.

"*Forty*," Keith said. And then he sighed and added, "The one to watch out for, I guess."

"You survived it," Ryan reminded him of his own fortieth two birthdays ago.

"You know, Ryan…" Keith began tenderly to his son, "you may think you're out on your own and learning a lot about women these days, but take my word for it…you ain't never going to learn enough about them."

CHAPTER 22

Their voices blended beautifully as they sang happy birthday to Carla. And there could be no better music to her ears. Keith, Ryan, and Jessie stood with her at the kitchen table, which held a big, decorated cake, honoring her with their song and their togetherness.

She hadn't known when she got up that morning, at the turn of forty years old, that there would be a party for her that day. But the kids came home. Jessie, with her stuff, to stay. And Keith was full of big, secretive smiles. And the cake came out of hiding. And then everyone sang and cheered and hugged her. And soon Carla was crying. But the tears were of a different sort than any she'd shed in the last few weeks. They were of pure joy.

She was thinking that if this was what turning forty was like, she shouldn't have dreaded it. As it was not much different from when she'd turned ten. Sixteen. Thirty.

"Thanks, guys!" she told them at the close of the song. "What a surprise!"

"And there's presents," Jessie exclaimed. She disappeared into the living room and came back with her arms full of brightly-wrapped packages.

"I...I'm not sure I deserve all this."

"Hey, you don't know what's inside these yet," Ryan warned her.

Carla dabbed her eyes and laughed. "Okay, I get it...probably snakes and lizards and—"

"Actually a cane and a few tubes of Bengay," Keith joked.

Ryan stepped forth to give his mother another hug. "You're not getting old, Mom..."

"Thanks," she responded all too quickly.

"But," he laughed, "you sure as heck ain't getting any younger."

Carla gave him a swat.

Jessie excitedly suggested, "Open them. Open your gifts, Mom."

Though they looked too beautiful to undo, Carla began working on them one by one. From Jessie there was a yellow tee-shirt with the big number 40 on the front of it. And a second gift from her was an over-sized coffee mug filled with candy. From Ryan she received a cute gardening hat and some envelopes of assorted flower seeds.

When she started to take the last gift off the table, Keith snatched it away from her saying, "It's from me…for later."

Carla curiously watched him put the package onto a kitchen counter. "Later…okay…" she agreed.

"Anybody home?" came a shout along with a knock at the back door.

Nathan entered with Alice under his arm. "Hey! Do I smell birthday cake?"

Her parents showered Carla with hugs and kisses. And they, too, brought presents. The biggest one, to her, was their being together again.

"We were invited for cake," Alice said, "only if we promised to bring the ice cream…which we did." She held up a large round container of chocolate chip, Carla's favorite.

"Was this all your doings?" Carla gave Keith a slanted look.

"Depends," he said, "on whether you like it or not."

"I like it."

"It was my doings," he admitted.

Jessie helped her grandmother dish up plates of ice cream and cake. Ryan brought a couple extra chairs from the living room, and they all sat around the table to eat.

Carla's parents gave her a mauve-colored sweater and a pair of slippers.

"Cute outfit," Keith remarked. "Can't wait to see you in it."

Carla slapped him playfully.

Although it was the gift of family, more than the materialistic gifts, that made this occasion so special to Carla, she was helplessly distracted by Keith's mysterious package yet to be opened. Along with her curiosity, she couldn't help feeling a little edgy about it…like what could it possibly be that she couldn't open in front of the others?

"I've got one more gift for you, but it couldn't be wrapped," Nathan told her.

Carla's curiosity switched to him. "Okay," she laughed.

"Well, I know you've been job hunting to no success," he said. "So…I came up with an offer you might like. It's quite diverse from what you've been used to. Which could be a good thing, I think."

"What, Grandpa, what?" Jessie, more than Carla, was eager to hear.

Nathan asked Carla, "How'd you like to work for me?"

Her mouth dropped, and it took her a few moments to find any words at all. "You mean…*paint*?"

"Yep, that's what I mean."

"Why?"

Nathan shrugged. "Business is good. Could use another worker. And you're looking for a job. How about it?"

Carla looked to Keith.

"First I heard of it," he said.

"Painting houses?" she further verified with her dad.

"And whatever else needs painting by whoever hires us. You'd be good at it, Carla. And you'd get paid. And you'd have fun. Right, Keith?"

Keith laughed. "Can't think of a more fun job. Yeah, Carla, I think it might be good for you. For a while anyway."

She stood up from the table and stuck her hands on her hips. "You guys are *serious*?"

"They're serious," Alice vouched for them.

Carla wandered off to the living room by herself to think about it.

Ryan followed her but allowed her a couple minutes before offering, "Sounds good to me, Mom. I think you should take it."

She smiled at what he'd said. "When Grandpa offered *you* a job painting with him a year ago you turned him down."

"That's me. I already had grease monkey written all over me."

"You don't think I have any big dream-career written all over me?" she asked.

"This could be it. You just didn't know it till now."

She shook her head and smiled all the more at her handsome son. "Think you're pretty smart, don't you."

"I'm still learning. You've taught me a lot more than you know, Mom. Have I ever told you thanks?"

"Maybe not in so many words."

"I'm sure it can't be easy being a parent," he said, "and I'm sure there's no such thing as a *perfect* parent. But I think you've done a great job, Mom. I'm proud to be your son."

His appraisal meant the world to Carla. She hugged her grown-up son as if he were still a child.

The afternoon ran into suppertime. Nathan ordered pizza. Jessie was in her glory, having ice cream, cake and pizza all on the same day. Everyone was having a great time.

After a long game of Monopoly, and a wild hour of charades, the party broke up.

Ryan was first to say good night. On his way out, he took a moment to look back and forth between his grandfather and his sister. "It's going to be rather lonely at my place now."

"We could get you a cat," Alice teased him.

"Oh, I think he can do much better than that," Nathan said.

After Ryan left, Jessie said she had homework to do. Keith felt her forehead to see if she was sick. Everyone laughed and said good night to the girl. She gave Carla one more birthday hug, then went upstairs.

"We should go," Alice told Carla, after clearing the dishes off the table. "Happy, happy birthday, darling…and many, many more. Don't be afraid of hitting forty. It looks wonderful on you. You've got a lot to be thankful for and a lot to look forward to."

"I love you, Mom," Carla said, embracing her. "Thanks for coming over, and for the gifts, and…and for being you."

"Well, I don't know who else I could possibly be," Alice joked.

Nathan stepped forth to give his daughter a kiss and a good night hug. "Sorry I kind of went off the deep end over hearing where you came from."

"You mean from the stork?" Carla grinned child-like.

Fondly recognizing that familiar side of her, he clarified, "You came from someone much higher up than the stork, sweetheart. You came from God. Straight from God to your mother and me. And you were stuck with the two of us right from the start."

"Not anymore than I was stuck with *you*," she teased him.

Nathan smiled and hugged her tighter. "Aren't we lucky, the three of us?"

"I love you guys," Carla said.

"Does that mean you'll take the job I offered you?"

"Can I sleep on it?" she asked.

"Sure. Happy Birthday, Carly. Forty looks great on you. And those little lines by your eyes…well, you've earned them and—"

"Let's go," Alice said, pushing him toward the door.

As the two of them left, Nathan announced that it'd started raining. "But the forecast says sunshine for tomorrow, so see ya on the job, Keith."

"Alone at last," Keith whispered intimately to Carla. "How I've waited for this moment."

"Mmm…" she sighed, with more contentment than she'd felt in a long time.

Then she broke away from him and went to fetch her one last birthday gift off the counter. "I want to open this now, because you said later and it's later. Okay?"

"Okay."

"On the porch," she said.

He followed her there and they sat in the swing. It was getting dark. And it was quiet except for the sound of the soft rain pattering the overhead roof. Carla held Keith's gift on her lap.

"You're not very eager," he said of her delay.

"Oh, I am," she assured him. "I'm trying to guess what it might be. But I can't. I just can't imagine. You've been very secretive about this."

"Open it," he urged her.

She untied the ribbon and pulled off the paper wrapping. It was a book. A spiral-bound book entitled, *Always Know*. And then she read the author's name, *by Keith Wade*. "You…you wrote a book?"

He shrugged modestly. "Didn't take long. It was rather easy."

"*You wrote a book?*" Carla exclaimed.

"If you open it, you'll see."

She felt unable to go any further than staring at the cover of the book in her hands.

"Probably a collector's item," he joked, "since you've got the one and only copy."

"I don't believe this. I…Keith…when, how?"

"You'll understand when you read it."

She nervously opened the book on her lap. The first page was a repeat of the title and author, with the addition of today's date beneath it.

The second page read, *To Carla*. The third page read, *Speaking as a professional painter, and your loving husband, there's no mistake between us that can't be painted over.* That one single sentence was repeated over and over, all down the page and onto the next page and the next and the next, all the way to the end of the book.

"One hundred pages of the same thing," Keith verified.

Carla smiled, closed the book and clutched it to her chest. "I love it."

Keith grinned modestly. "Pretty easy writing, once I got the first sentence done."

"This book…it's exactly what I needed more than anything at this time. Thank you, honey. I love it. I love *you*."

"I know you do, Carla," he said. "I'd be pretty stupid to ever doubt that. Or to let *you* doubt it. That's why I wrote the book. There's never to be a doubt between us again."

"No," she agreed. "And…and you've gotta know how sorry I am about—"

"I do know," he assured her.

Suddenly Carla leaned away from him, struck with the curiosity of, "Where did you—"

"I, uh, had it printed at Milo Printing. By one of your ex-coworkers."

"Alonzo? You dealt with Alonzo?"

"I dealt with him, yes. He wasn't so bad to deal with. I didn't hit him or anything. I…I just took in my one typed page and my specifications for the book binding. And after he took my order, he took my *warning*. Which I won't share with you. It…was a man-to-man thing."

Carla felt somewhere between laughing and crying.

Keith put his arms around her. "Oh, Carla…life can get so messed up and complicated sometimes. But this book…I intend it to be a constant reminder to you, *to us*, how very deep true love is. I mean…if it's there, really there, then it's there forever, no matter what."

"I love the book, Keith. I'm totally amazed and touched by it. You are one special guy, you know that?"

"I know," he said. "You're pretty special, too, Carla. Even though you *are* getting old."

She moaned and gave him a playful jab in the side. They shared a laugh and soon they were sharing a kiss.

Nathan had been right about the weather report. Though it'd rained a good part of the night, morning brought the sun—a beautiful follow-up to Carla's fortieth birthday party. He stood bursting with smiles and shaking his head as she and Keith walked toward him and the house that was today's job site.

Carla was wearing a pair of old blue jeans, topped with one of Keith's white paint shirts rolled under and tied at her waist. And here she was…with a new job, a new boss, a new coworker, a new place in her life. Maybe life would never be as sweet and simple as it'd been for her before the chain of events that started that one Friday night, but she'd learned that she and her family had the love and strength to withstand them.

Nathan handed Carla an open can of paint and Keith handed her a brush. She gave her dad a kiss, and her husband a kiss, and her paintbrush a kiss. Then she headed for the side of the house that was to be the starting point of her new job and her new life.

And she loved it.

Correspondence to the author should be addressed to:

Marilyn DeMars

P.O. Box 28234

Crystal, MN 55428

978-0-595-40665-4
0-595-40665-3

NORMANDALE COMMUNITY COLLEGE
LIBRARY
9700 FRANCE AVENUE SOUTH
BLOOMINGTON, MN 55431-4399